The Hall of the Singing Caryatids

The Hall
of the Singing Caryatids

•

VICTOR PELEVIN

Translated by Andrew Bromfield

A NEW DIRECTIONS PEARL

Copyright © 2008 Victor Pelevin
Translation copyright © 2011 Andrew Bromfield
Copyright © 2011 New Directions

"The Hall of the Singing Caryatids," originally published in Russia as "Зал по-
   ющих кариатид," appeared in Pelevin's 2008 collection П5: прощальные
   песни политических пигмеев Пиндостана [*P5: Farewell songs of the political pygmies of Pindostan*] by arrangement with the author and the Nicole Aragi Agency.

Manufactured in the United States of America
New Directions Books are printed on acid-free paper.
First published as a Pearl (NDP1214) by New Directions in 2011
Published simultaneously in Canada by Penguin Books Canada Limited
Design by Erik Rieselbach
Set in Albertina and Frutiger

Library of Congress Cataloging-in-Publication Data

Pelevin, Viktor.
[Zal pojuwih kariatid. English]
The hall of the singing caryatids / Victor Pelevin ; translated from the Russian by
   Andrew Bromfield. — 1st American pbk. ed.
p. cm.
"A New Directions Pearl."
ISBN 978-0-8112-1942-6 (paperbook : acid-free paper) — ISBN 978-0-8112-1953-2
   (ebook)
I. Bromfield, Andrew. II. Title.
PG3485.E38Z3313 2011
891.73'44—dc23

                                      2011023260

10 9 8 7 6 5 4 3 2 1

New Directions Books are published for James Laughlin
by New Directions Publishing Corporation
80 Eighth Avenue, New York, NY 10011

THE HALL
OF THE SINGING CARYATIDS

LENA ARRIVED FOR THE AUDITION TWO HOURS ahead of the scheduled time, but she was still only ninth in line.

The girls who had gathered among the yellow leather, glass, chrome, and vintage Hollywood posters that decorated the walls of the small foyer instead of paintings were evidently nervous.

Lena was too.

The girls disappeared through a pebble-glass door at an approximate rate of one every fifteen minutes, then emerged and walked to the exit. Their faces gave absolutely nothing away.

When the electronic chime rang out in the foyer and the secretary called her name, Lena panicked and took so long stuffing her book into her purse that the secretary actually pressed the button again. But Lena recovered her self-control on her way to the pebble-glass door, and pushed it open with a steady hand.

Inside was a small office that looked like a cosmetic surgeon's front office: a desk, a couple of armchairs, and a hard medical couch upholstered in imitation leather. The owner of the office, commonly known as "Uncle Pete," was sitting on the couch with his hairy legs crossed, smoking a cigar. Uncle Pete was a chubby man of about fifty, with a naked cranium and a fleshy face, sporting stylish rectangular glasses. Although he was freshly shaved, he gave the impression of being unshaven: his greying stubble was so invincibly thick, it looked as if he had sprinkled the ash from his cigar over his head and then, to complete his penitence, rubbed a certain amount of ash into his cheeks. He was dressed like a child—in crumpled white shorts and a t-shirt with a rainbow-bright slogan:

TALIBAN ICHKERIA

He gazed at Lena for a while, chewing on his cigar, then pointed to the desk and said:

"Take your clothes off and climb up.... No, I mean the other way around. Climb up and take your clothes off."

Lena had been aware that she would have to sing naked, but she was shocked to realize it was all going to happen on a desk in a smoky, poky little room. That just didn't seem serious, somehow. But on the other hand, this place was about as serious as they come, and she knew it.

This manifest incongruity could mean only one thing—her idea of what was serious and what wasn't didn't correspond to the true reality. But that kind of thing had happened to her before. And so, casting her doubts aside, she climbed up on the desk and quickly stripped.

"Sing," said Uncle Pete.

"I've got a keydrive with music," Lena replied. "Is there anywhere to put it?"

"Let's do it without music."

Lena had prepared a song for just this contingency, one that the t.A.T.u. girls sang, about Yugoslavia—it was a great vehicle for her thin, clear voice. Lena started singing:

The Danube in the evening is flooded with
White light, white light, white light …

"Lift one leg," said Uncle Pete.

Lena blushed but went on singing as she raised her left leg, keeping it bent at the knee. It was awkward standing on one leg, but she could manage it. She spread her arms wide and tried to make her pose as elegant as possible.

The feeling of shame lent her voice a certain piercing, crystal clarity. Uncle Pete didn't even look at her—well, maybe he gave her a couple of sideways glances. He was preoccupied with his cigar, which had burned down too rapidly on one side. He anxiously anointed the trouble spot with saliva and puffed streams of smoke up toward the ceiling, but he still couldn't get the cigar to burn evenly.

When Lena sang "You are leaving, consumed by the flames, Yugoslavia, without me without me without me," it seemed to trigger some kind of content-addressable relay in Uncle Pete's head. He shook the ash off his cigar, frowned, and said:

"That's enough. Let's have something else."

"And can I put my leg down?" Lena asked

Uncle Pete shook his head. By this time Lena was pretty tired, and she made a mistake.

She started singing Nautilus Pompilius's "Wheels of

Love." It was a beautiful song, but it had an elusive, gliding kind of motif; she should really only have sung it with music.

"Eve and Adam, they both knew, the wheels of love roll on through…," she began, but after a few seconds she squawked such an obviously false note that she stopped in embarrassment, then started again.

"Don't bother," Uncle Pete told her.

He put his cigar down on the edge of the couch and quickly jotted something down in a notepad.

"Can I lower my leg?" Lena asked again.

"Sure," Uncle Pete said with a nod. "You can get dressed already."

"What about the recitation? Aren't you going to listen to the recitation?"

"No."

Lena got down off the desk. She felt a red flush of shame on her cheeks, and there was nothing she could do about it. As she got dressed, she gazed self-consciously into the trash can—as if she had accepted that that was where she belonged from now on.

•

Uncle Pete called a week later, when Lena had already gotten over it. The call came early in the morning. Lena's sister, who answered the phone, said: "Some hotshot looking for you".

Lena didn't realize who it was at first, but when Uncle Pete called her "Yugoslavia" she guessed she must have passed the audition.

"I never had any doubts about you," Uncle Pete told her. "The moment you lifted that leg, I knew.... Are you free this afternoon?"

"Yes," said Lena. "Of course."

"Know where the Radisson-Slavyanskaya Hotel is? Be there, at the entrance, at three, and bring your passport. You'll see someone there holding a placard that says 'semiotic signs.' Go up to them."

"Why?"

"Because, my dumb little dolly, the person with the placard will take you where you need to go. Were you expecting something bad? Don't you worry, there's no more bad stuff to come. Only good stuff and really good stuff. Unless, of course, you forget how to blush. That's the most important thing in our business..."

And Uncle Pete laughed.

Lena was there at a quarter to three.

It looked as if the Slavyanskaya Hotel was hosting some event of enormous importance for global semiotics—there were several women in hotel uniforms standing at the doors, holding those placards in their hands. One of them checked a list and led Lena to the business center, where a whole crowd of semiotic boys and girls had already gathered—it reminded her a bit of September and the first day of school.

Another woman in a uniform delivered Lena to a little, semi-circular conference room with black armchairs. It was clearly intended for small, private presentations.

Some girls she'd never seen before were sitting there. By force of habit, Lena went to the back row and sat down next to a petite girl with an Asiatic slant to her eyes who looked completely Japanese.

"Asya," the Japanese girl introduced herself, smiling so enchantingly that Lena immediately realized the other girl had also passed the audition.

"Lena," said Lena, shaking the outstretched hand. "What's going to happen now?"

"I heard it's some kind of introductory session."

Lena looked round at the gathering. In all, there were twelve girls in the small conference room—they were all beautiful, but different, as if they had been specially selected for contrasting types of physical appeal that would reinforce the overall impact. There were two black girls, one mulatto, two dusky girls from Central Asia, two with narrow, slanting eyes (Asya was more beautiful than the other one), and five generally European-looking girls: three blondes (Lena included herself), one brunette, and one with chestnut hair.

After a few minutes of waiting, Uncle Pete entered the room, wearing a brown, double-breasted jacket over a black turtleneck sweater. He was accompanied by a young man with dark hair wearing a grey Zegna suit and a tie of such a discreetly elegant shade that any lingering doubts Lena might have had about the seriousness of what was happening were laid to rest once and for all.

Uncle Pete was clearly not the senior partner in this duo: he treated the young man very obsequiously, turning the microphone on for him and even brushing non-existent dust off his chair.

After seating himself at the microphone, the young man looked round at the girls, smiled sadly, and started speaking.

"You know what's going on in the world right now, don't you, girls? The geopolitical confrontation between civilizations based on service to the principles of spirit or of matter has intensified to the ultimate degree. This is the result of that same secret tension of forces as in that early morning before the Battle of Kulikovo Field, when the Orthodox host awaited its hour of the star and the cross...."

The young man glanced round sternly at the girls, as if he were hinting at who the Orthodox host would be this time around—but Lena had already figured that out ages ago. Although that "star and cross" business wasn't clear—she thought it must be a kind of loan-translation from the Americanism "stars and stripes," a response to the dictatorship of McDonald's, filched for lack of a decent copywriter, but leavened with a correct spiritual principle.

"The situation is rendered particularly acute," the young man continued, "by the fact that in the course of a predatory and criminal process of privatization, the wealth of our country fell into the hands of a bunch of oligarchs specially selected—by agents operating in the dark wings of the international stage—on the basis of their spiritual squalor. Not that they were irredeemably bad people, no, you shouldn't think that, papa mama nuthouse eighteen. They were more like little children, incapable of striving for any goal except the satisfaction of their constantly shifting desires. Hence all those soccer clubs, giant yachts, twenty-thousand-Euro bottles of wine, and other ghastly aberrations, about which I think you have already heard more than enough...."

Lena didn't understand what "papa mama nuthouse eighteen" meant (the young man had muttered those words rapidly and quietly), but she forgot about that right away—she suddenly wanted so badly to take a sip of twenty-thousand-Euros-a-bottle wine that her mouth started watering. A quiet sigh ran round the room, confirming that the girls had not only heard a lot about these aberrations but had actually studied in minute detail every bit of available information.

"In recent times the intelligence agencies of the West have launched a genuine manhunt for our wealthy goofballs," the young man continued. "You have heard, of course, about the notorious scandals and arrests: first Courchevel, then Fiji, then the Hermès boutique, and now St. Moritz, the Maldives, and Antarctica. This carefully planned campaign has pursued two fundamental goals—first, to discredit Russian civilization, and second, to establish control over Russia's resources by gathering compromising material about the owners of the country's basic assets. Our elite has become a target, and the objective reality of the current point in the space-time continuum is such that *we* have become a target together with it."

He frowned and stopped speaking, as if giving his listeners a chance to appreciate the full seriousness of the situation. Then the sad smile reappeared on his face and he continued:

"We have to get the situation under control. What does this require? In the first instance, we must create conditions in which these infantile knuckleheads can no longer disgrace our country abroad. We must, so to speak, recreate here, on our side of the border, the stupefying mirage that attracts them to the West. Thus we shall ensure the security of the Fatherland's strategic reserves and at the same time retain, here in Russia, the immense financial resources that the oligarchs waste on their perverse pastimes. This, we can say, is one of today's absolutely top-priority national projects—although, for obvious reasons, you won't hear a single word about it on TV."

He looked at his watch.

"My friend Pyotr here will tell you the rest. The most important thing you must realize is that, despite the apparent—ambivalence, let us say—of your work, it is every bit as important as a tour of duty in a nuclear submarine that forms part of our nation's defensive shield. Perhaps even more important, because today's war is not the war of fifty years ago, and it is fought with quite different means. The country needs a new kind of defensive shield, one that protects our frontiers from within, and you girls will be the ones to bear it! Today the cause of Alexander Nevsky becomes your cause! This is an immense responsibility, but also a great honor. And on this journey, may your hearts be illuminated by the inexpressibly beautiful principle that Borya Grebenshchikov refers to as 'the Work of Master Bo'—which simple folk like myself call 'the transcendental extralinguistic imperative.' Everything depends on you now. Good luck!"

The young man whispered something in Uncle Pete's ear, stood up, waved good-bye with his elegant little hand, and walked out of the room.

"Did you all understand what he was talking about?" Uncle Pete asked, staring up eloquently at the ceiling. "Yes … well then. He used to be an éminence grise. No one ever saw him in person. But now he speaks in public on all sorts of subjects, he communes with the people. A genuine democrat, by the way, in the best sense—he arrived in a plain, unpimped BMW. But I strongly advise you not to talk about this conversation with anyone else."

Lena didn't understand what an éminence grise was, but she decided not to ask anybody about it—in case she accidentally gave something away.

"Get this into your heads right now," Uncle Pete continued. "In your job you need more than just long legs, you need a short memory. No one—not your mom, or your dad, or your little brother, or even the priest at confession—must know what happens while you're working. I think you already understand the consequences of any breach of this principle. Or is there anyone who still hasn't figured that out?"

Uncle Pete looked around the hushed hall.

"Have we just joined a spy school, then?" one of the girls asked.

"Near enough," Uncle Pete said with a smile. "Do you think we're playing with buckets and spades here? If you leaf through glossies from the last few years, you'll see your Uncle Pete here is always complaining to the society columnists that he never gets any orders for girls from the Rublyovskoe Chaussee, all his clients are in the provinces nowadays. Of course, we pay the columnists, and the magazines. We're working intensively on public opinion, implanting the idea that in the contemporary oligarch's system of values the family comes first, a foreign education for his children comes second, and Orthodox ideals come in a close third, but nowadays debauchery is really old hat. Serious resources are being devoted to that effort, girls. But just imagine one of you starts trading in nookie.... The entire edifice collapses. Do you understand the consequences?"

"Everybody understands that already," a blonde with short-cropped hair sitting in the front row said in a man's voice. "Let's hear something constructive. Where are we going to work?"

"Under the Rublyovka."

"You mean, close to the Rublyovka?"

Uncle Pete shook his head and pointed down at the floor.

"What does that mean?" the blonde asked tensely.

"You'll be working in a complex that is currently being completed close to the Rublyovskoe Chaussee. It is located a thousand feet underground and can withstand a direct hit by a nuclear bomb. The complex will act as a bomb shelter for the national elite in the case of war or terrorist attacks. In peacetime it will be an exclusive recreation center that the elite can visit confidentially, without even leaving their own neighborhood."

"You mean no one's going to know about this shelter?" Asya asked.

"It's not easy to keep construction work on this scale secret," Uncle Pete replied, "but it's quite possible to keep what's going to happen there secret. All the staff, including you, will know only what concerns them directly. And by the way, don't go thinking that now you're the bee's knees. You are by no means the most important element of the project. You're not even USAS."

"What do you mean by USAS?" one of the girls asked.

"A USA is a Unit of Sexual Attraction," Uncle Pete replied. "Our professional jargon."

"Then who are we?"

"You are simply a decorative element in one of the auxiliary areas. You are Singing Caryatids. Do you know what that is?"

Not everybody did—that much was clear from their faces.

Uncle Pete was obviously feeling hot—he took off his jacket and hung it on the back of his chair. Down at stomach level on his black turtleneck was a picture of a spermatozoid curved into the Nike squiggle with the caption:

JUST DID IT

"The dictionary of the Russian language," said Uncle Pete, "tells us that the word 'caryatid' signifies a sculpture of a woman that acts as a support for a roof or appears to perform this function.... What is meant by 'acting as a support for a roof' has just been explained to you, that's the political aspect. But now we're going to talk about what 'appearing to perform that function' means. We are creating an entirely new type of personal pleasure zone. Its fundamental, distinctive stylistic element will be the naked female body. Of course, that doesn't mean a room full of naked broads. No one nowadays is interested in some Neapolitan tarantella, the kind of thing once mocked so viciously by the writer Averchenko. No.... What we are doing here will outdo anything that even the decadent Roman emperors ever witnessed."

Uncle Pete leaned his body back, assuming an air of Roman decadence. In Lena's opinion, it was highly convincing—even with the rectangular glasses.

"Imagine caryatids," he continued, "who come to life when the client wishes, who engage him in conversation and provide him with various services of an intimate nature ... but only if the client is interested. The rest of the time they remain petrified, they are merely a detail of an interior in which absolutely anything can happen—from a sophisticated orgy to a shareholders' meeting. If he wishes, a client can bring his girls to this space, or even his family, and then you will have to maintain your stony immobility. Or perhaps perform a few vocal numbers to provide background music."

"And how are we going to maintain our stony immobility for hours on end?" asked the short-cropped blonde in the front row. "Is the Motherland going to teach us?"

"Don't get cute, kitten," replied Uncle Pete. "That's exactly what She will do, tomorrow morning. Only first She'll get you to sign an agreement."

"Not to leave the country?" asked the blonde.

Uncle Pete smiled.

"A nondisclosure agreement. Forget those horrors from your childhood."

•

There were three men waiting in the gym—one in a white coat with a beard, one a major of some dappled branch of the armed forces, and a weary-looking, bald man in a tracksuit. The doctor in the white coat looked like a good-natured Doolittle, but the major more than compensated for the doctor's good nature—his face looked like a brick that been used to smash dozens of skulls, and it wasn't making any promises.

He started the meeting by forming the girls up in a line.

"Concerning secrecy," he said, looking down vaguely in

the direction of his crotch, "I wanted to show you a film of two lousy snitches being burned alive in a furnace. My superiors wouldn't allow it. I suggest you take my word that such things happen. Do you believe me?"

Lena was standing first in line, so she felt she ought to answer.

"We believe you, Comrade Major. Yesterday they really hammered all this secrecy stuff into our heads."

"They hammered one thing into your heads," said the major, "but I'm hammering something else. What you go telling the glam journalists about your fancy fucks from the Rublyovka has nothing to do with me. But what I'm about to show you now is classified information, with 'Top Secret' stamped all over it, and you're responsible for keeping it that way."

He walked over to a tennis bag lying by the wall and took out a trashy grey cardboard box—like the ones they use to pack spare parts for all sorts of boring machines. The box contained a nickel-plated injection gun and a roll of ampoules packed in plastic.

Lena was standing close and she could see every detail: the triangular heads of the ampoules made them look like bullets, and the roll looked like a machine-gun belt. The ampoules had nothing written on them, just some little red marks on the side. The liquid in them was tea-colored.

"This serum is called Mantis-B," said the major. "It was developed in 1985 for the Special Forces. The comrade colonel will tell you all about it."

Lena was expecting the weary man in the tracksuit to

speak but, to her surprise, it was Dr. Doolittle who answered to the name of Comrade Colonel. He clasped his hands together on his stomach, narrowed his eyes, and began:

"As you have already been told girls, this serum is called Mantis-B. In Greek, 'mantis' means 'prophet.' It is also the biological name of an insect, known as the praying mantis because it holds its spiky front limbs together in front of its chest, like hands clasped in prayer. The praying mantis is a very interesting insect; the only one that can turn its head. It has numerous eyes...."

"Get to the important part, Comrade Colonel," said the major. "You'll exhaust us all with these zoological details."

"All right. Basically we're only interested in one special feature of this insect. While lying in wait for its prey, the praying mantis can remain motionless for hours. Its coloring and form resemble a dry twig, so other insects approach it without fear. And that's when the mantis grabs them with its spiky front limbs...."

Dr. Doolittle grabbed something invisible, raised his hands to his mouth, and loudly gnashed his teeth together. A nervous titter ran through the group, and it occurred to Lena that the doctor's good-natured appearance served the same function as the mantis's resemblance to a dry twig.

"Our specialists," the doctor went on, "spent many years investigating the paranormal features of numerous animals and insects. They studied mantises in an attempt to understand how this insect can remain totally immobile for such long periods. You've seen movies about Japanese Ninjas, so you understand how useful this could be, for instance to a sniper waiting in ambush or a secret service agent—especially these days, when any security system includes highly sensitive motion detectors. Our research led to the isolation from the mantis's brain and nervous system of the substance responsible for this mechanism. It is a complex protein, a rather distant analog of a toxin, or rather, repressor, consisting of a dual-domain globule of bonded disulphide..."

"Comrade Colonel," the major said reproachfully.

The doctor nodded.

"Well basically," he continued, "the Mantis-B serum was created from this substance. It allows a human being to remain totally immobile for hours on end without any adverse physiological effects. Let me emphasize that—total, stony immobility."

"They won't understand," said the major. "They have to be shown. Vasyok, come over here."

The man in the tracksuit walked dutifully over to the major.

"Show them your hands," the doctor ordered.

Vasyok held his hands out in front of him. They were trembling visibly.

"You can put them down now."

The major took an ampoule out of the plastic ribbon, loaded it into the injection gun, and said edgily: "Well, crouch down already!"

Vasyok got down on his knees. The major put the injection gun to the back of his neck and pressed the release catch. There was a sharp hiss and Vasyok said:

"Agh! That's cold!"

"When injected into the occipital region, the effect is practically instantaneous," said the doctor.

Vasyok got to his feet.

"Show them your hands again," said the doctor.

Vasyok obeyed. The fingers were now perfectly still.

The doctor thought for a moment before parting Vasyok's arms and raising them into the air. Then he inclined the man's body, forcing him to lift one foot off the ground. Vasyok assumed the pose of a statue holding an amphora—leaning forward and balancing with one leg stretched out behind him—and froze.

Lena felt the unreality of what was happening more keenly with every passing second. Despite the evident instability of the pose, Vasyok stood as still and steady as a rock—his hands and raised leg didn't make the slightest movement. But the most astounding thing was the change that occurred in his face. Lena had just been looking at the guilty features of an alcoholic—twitchy, tense, wrinkled simultaneously into several grimaces, overlaid one on top of the other. What she now saw before her was the face of a saint, with all the muscles relaxed in an expression of absolute calm and trust, looking beautiful, despite his wrinkles.

"Impossible...." whispered one of the girls in the line.

The colonel in the white coat smiled contentedly.

"How long do you think he can stand like that? An hour? Two? Ha ha! Up to two and a half days! And at the same time he will remain lucidly aware of everything and capable of communicating. Only I advise you not to drink too much water before your shift. Vasyok, how are you feeling?"

The saint opened his eyes and said:

"Just fine, Comrade Colonel. Only my shorts are pinching a bit."

•

The short-cropped blonde was named Vera. She lived near Profsoyuznaya metro station, while Lena and Asya lived quite close to each other in Belyaevo. They all rode the metro home together, got out at Profsoyuznaya, and set off into the street.

"There's something I don't like about all this," said Lena. "I thought it would be a high-end cabaret with special extras for exclusive clients. But this is some kind of circus. "Caryatids."

"You know," Vera answered, "for this kind of money I'd work as a car-jack, never mind a caryatid. My father's an alcoholic; at night I push my desk against the door to keep him out. I need my own apartment."

"And what do you think?" Lena asked Asya.

Asya smiled her wonderful Japanese smile.

"I think it's quite interesting, really," she said. "And in any case it's certainly better than being ordinary prostitutes."

That sounded so artless that all three of them laughed.

"Listen," said Lena, "This is what I'd like to know: If we're going to work on the Rublyovka, will they give us a place to live there?"

"Oh sure, fat chance," Vera replied. "Uncle Pete said something about taking us in a bus."

"Every day?"

"No. We'll be working in three shifts of four girls. Two days on, four days off. That's why they took twelve of us."

"That's fine," said Asya. "It's like being a conductor of a train. Girls, why don't we ask to be on the same shift?"

"What for?"

"We live near each other," said Asya. "We can get the bus to come to Profsoyuznaya station, instead of trudging all the way over to the Slavyanskaya Hotel."

"That's an idea," Vera agreed. "But we'll have to find someone else who lives here."

"Look at that!" said Lena. A car appeared from around the corner—a long, white stretch limo. It was so long, it could hardly even negotiate the bend, and its dark-tinted windows excluded any hope of penetrating them to infringe upon someone else's privacy. The limousine was like a reconnaissance craft that had descended from some happy empyrean realm into a low orbit below dark clouds, into the grey world of economic expediency, efficiency, and the gnashing of teeth. It was obvious that the reconnaissance mission would soon come to an end, and the craft would fly back to where it had come from. But its appearance was more than a mere hint at other people's prosperity and happiness, it also inspired a timid hope: the roof was adorned with two gold rings that looked like a radar locator.

Lena ran her gaze over the black windows and white enameled door, then lowered her eyes to the glittering nickel-plated hubcaps, surrounded by black rubber. She realized these were the very same wheels of love that she had sung about at the audition.

"The important thing now is not to hit any flat notes," she murmured.

"What?" asked Vera.

"Nothing," said Lena. "Just something I remembered."

·

The fourth to join their shift was a black girl called Kima. She lived near the next metro stop, Akademicheskaya, and agreed to meet the others at Profsoyuznaya.

Kima turned out to be the best educated and brightest of the girls. Almost too bright, really. After talking to her a couple of times, Lena was quite disgruntled to realize her own ignorance in matters of contemporary culture: before they met, she had genuinely believed that the artist Kulik had earned a fortune by chirping like a bird, and that "shvydkoi" was a Ukrainian term of abuse with a vile anti-Semitic aftertaste, not the surname of the head of the Federal Agency for Culture and Cinematography.

And on top of all that, Kima had a funny way of saying hello—she struck herself on her left shoulder with her right fist and said:

"Putin morgen!"

Meeting at Profsoyuznaya was convenient, because the black Mercedes minibus with the placard that said "semiotic signs" set off at seven in the morning. It would have been a pain to get up early enough to catch it somewhere in the center of town.

On the first trip, they were all nervous. Kima seemed particularly somber.

"I have a bad feeling about this," she said when the minibus set off. "I think we've been duped. This is some kind of crap, not a serious project."

"Why?" asked Asya.

"Well, take that notice in the window," said Kima. "Semiotic signs. That's already enough to give me the shakes. Semiotics is the science of sign systems, we covered it at university. Translate it into normal Russian and you get 'sign signs.' That's enough to make anyone with an education laugh."

"Aha," muttered Asya, who was also in a foul mood. "So it would be better if they wrote 'whorish prostitutes?'"

Lena frowned.

"We're not prostitutes, she said. "We're more like geishas, really. We sing. We recite."

"Oh yeah, not just a plain glory hole," said Asya. "There's

a pair of earphones and a soundtrack as well. So the price is different."

Kima raised her finger.

"Thanks for reminding me. Uncle Pete's personal assistant called yesterday, he said to put together a list of songs, so they could set up a recording session. For the accompaniment, I mean—they won't let us lip-synch. He said all they needed was twenty to thirty numbers. We'll have just enough time to do it on the way."

The driver turned out to have a datebook with weekly pages, and he allowed them to tear out a few clean ones. Incredibly enough, all four of them had "Wheels of Love" in their sets.

Lena had prudently brought the printout of her repertoire, as prepared for the audition, so she didn't have to write anything. She could relax.

She took the driver's well-thumbed copy of *Eligible Bachelors of Russia* magazine. Inside it was another slim, badly tattered magazine, titled *Counterculture*. It wasn't clear if this was a separate publication or simply a supplement. *Counterculture* was printed on poor quality newsprint and looked very dubious, even sordid, but Vera explained that that was deliberate.

"It's counterculture," she said, as if the word explained everything.

"And what's that?" Lena asked.

"That's when they use dirty words on cheap paper,"

Vera explained. "So they can badmouth the glossies. It's hot shit nowadays."

Asya frowned.

"That's not right," she said, "it doesn't have to be on cheap paper, sometimes the paper's expensive. Counterculture's …" She hesitated for a moment, as if she was trying to recall a phrase that she'd heard somewhere. "It's the aesthetic of anti-bourgeois revolt, expropriated by the ruling elite, that's what it is."

"But how can you expropriate an aesthetic?" Vera asked.

"No problem," replied Asya. "Nowadays, everyone who's got a competent PR manager is a rebel. Any dumb bitch on TV can say she's on the run from the FSB.… I don't get you girls; I don't see why we should have any complexes about the job. Because everyone's a prostitute nowadays, even the air—for letting the radio waves pass through it."

"You take such an emotional view of everything, seeing it all with your heart," said Kima. "You won't last long like that. And anyway, that's not what counterculture is."

"Then what is it?" asked Asya.

"It's just a market niche," Kima replied with a shrug. "And not just here, it's the same all over the world. Think of it—'counter'—counterculture is any commodity someone's hoping to sell big-time, so they put it on the checkout counter. Lena, why are you so quiet?"

"I'm reading," Lena replied. "I don't understand why they use dotted lines for profanity, if they're in revolt."

"That's to attract more readers."

"Aha. And here they write: 'a brilliant intellectual, experimenting within the mainstream …' Is that counterculture?"

"No," said Asya. "That's one cute guy on the make and another one doing his PR."

Lena didn't ask any more questions, but she was still wondering what counterculture really was, and decided to read right through the supplement.

She half listened to the girls with one ear as she read the lead article: "The 100 Most Expensive Wh…s in Moscow (with Phone Numbers and Addresses)"— followed by the comments on it (one commentator wrote in to ask why was that Drozdovets, the host of the popular talk show "Hats Off!," wasn't in the list—was it because of a sudden moral transformation or a temporary decline in his ratings?). Then she frowned at a strange advertisement ("Weary of the hustle and bustle of the city? In just two minutes, you can be in a pine forest. Washing lines from the Free Space factory!"), leafed through an article about the singer Shnurkov ("Why, of all the warriors doing battle against the dictatorship of the manager, was this sophisticated Che Guevara, known to many well-to-do gentlemen for his scintillating songs at exclusive corporate events, the first to point out that he was no slouch when it came to picking up on the ringtone? Because he realized that these days it's the only way to get *his* ringtone playing on *your* iPhone, dear manager!"), then Lena read an interview with Shnurkov himself ("The composer of

'Ham..r that C..t' and 'D..k in a Con..m' reflects on the trends and metamorphoses of contemporary Russian cinema"), and then—probably because of the tiresome countercultural profanities—she started feeling depressed and lonely, so she closed the supplement and dived into the quiet, glossy waters of *Eligible Bachelors of Russia*.

Immediately she came across a large article titled "The Last Russian Macho." It was devoted to the oligarch Botvinik, whom it called "Russia's No. 1 Eligible Bachelor." Lena peered, gimlet-eyed, at the photo of a stocky, chubby individual with an unnatural, bright blush right across his cheeks—as if she were trying to drill a fishing hole in the glossy surface and hook the key to some kind of secret code out of it.

"Could you love someone like that?" Asya asked, glancing into the magazine.

"Why not?" replied Lena. "You can always find something good in anyone. And when someone has a few billion dollars, you can find an awful lot of something good. You just have to look for it."

Kima got up off her seat to take a look at the photo.

"Try talking to him with your thoughts," she said. "I heard that you can attract someone by looking at his photo and talking to it. But you have to promise him something that will make him want to see you too. Then you're bound to meet in real life."

Lena thanked her sardonically and started reading....

•

She learned a lot of interesting things from the article:

It recalled the absolutely prehistoric rumor that Botvinik had smashed Jean-Claude Van Damme's face in at a disco in Monte Carlo during the nineties, and how he supposedly couldn't go abroad again for a long time, because he was wanted by Interpol. She didn't really believe it—at that time Lena's older sister was having a fling with a thug from Orekhovo-Zuevo, so ever since she was just a kid, Lena had known how difficult it was to find a thug from Orekhovo-Zuevo who hadn't smashed Jean-Claude Van Damme's face in at a disco in Monte Carlo (many of them used to hint with an obscene sneer that things had gone further than that). If Interpol had ever been looking for Botvinik then, of course, it was for something else— but the overworked rumor, on which all the serious political pundits had eagerly commented ("The West has been given yet another reason to gnash its teeth in frustration"), was itself an indication of such vast financial resources that it was far classier than actually smashing Jean-Claude Van Damme's face in.

And the article hinted at that. One of the photos showed the oligarch on a deserted beach, with a tattoo of a bat clearly visible on his shoulder (that section of the shot was reproduced, greatly enlarged, alongside).

There was a shady story to that bat....

According to one version, Botvinik had served in the

paratroopers (one photograph showed him in uniform, with his arms around some guys in blue berets outside the entrance to Gorky Park on Army Day), and the symbol had been tattooed on him following the paratroopers' tradition. But according to another version he had simply been the first Russian oligarch to consider what later became known as PR, and invested in his public image before anyone else. So during the loans-for-shares auctions, articles in the *Kommersant* newspaper about his financial operations were actually titled "The Paratroopers Have Landed." Supposedly, however, he actually had the bat tattoo done later, when a exposé appeared on Dirt.ru about him never having been in the army.

The subject of "Russian machismo" derived from the same origin—the author of the article commented on the irony that Botvinik was not naturally suited to this role, having been raised by his parents as a decent, cultured individual. But even so, a specially assembled team of cultural analysts, psychologists, and specialists in neuro-linguistic programming (NLP) had helped him achieve a total self-transformation, in the process developing for him the technique of "Crypto-Speak"—a conversational strategy that implants special microcommands in another person's consciousness. These microcommands were harmless enough in themselves, but in the context of a precisely calibrated phrase they effectively constituted a binary linguistic weapon. In combination with rigorously exact gestures, they affected the subconscious in such a way that a few minutes of interaction was enough for Botvinik to subjugate any typical Russian to his will.

Not much was known about Crypto-Speak. It was believed that, in addition to exploiting traditional cultural codes, it made use of command-memes assembled in accordance with kabbalistic principles out of letter-and-digit combinations disguised as everyday speech. This tool of psychological influence had proved stunningly effective—so effective that it had been classified and added to the armory of the major political technologists, many of whom regarded Botvinik as their guru.

Crypto-Speak's greatest secret was the specific technology Combat NLP—but all information on this subject had been hidden away so securely that the author of the article didn't even try to guess at the meaning of the term. Botvinik was the pioneer in this area—a mastery of Crypto-Speak in combination with Combat NLP was believed to be one of the main reasons for his devastating business success. Another was that Botvinik supposedly held the rank of colonel in the KGB (the author of the article doubted the accuracy of this rumor, but he was sure that Botkin managed the state security slush fund through a subsidiary company in the City of London.

"It might seem strange to a nonprofessional that the Litvinenko scandal and the conflict in the Caucasus have had little impact on all these circumstances," the magazine article said. "In fact, the financial integration of various elite groups is one of the concealed balance beams that prevent the world from tipping over into total chaos: no antiballistic missile system can better defend you against a rusty nuclear bomb than a convivial understanding of the way things work."

In recent years Botvinik had been living mostly in London (Interpol had clearly dropped its claims about Jean-Claude Van Damme), but he often visited Moscow.

It was an interesting article, but a bit too highbrow: some phrases seemed like total gibberish to Lena, even though they consisted of words that she understood. For instance: "In modern Russia, ideologies have been displaced by technologies, which means that Botvinik, who fronted the new generation of neurolinguistic technicians, can quite legitimately be called both the supreme technologist for all the ideologists and the supreme ideologist for all the technologists ..." Lena read this part through again twice, but she still didn't understand what it was all about.

"Combat NLP," she repeated in a whisper and looked at Botvinik's flushed cheeks.

It occurred to her that Kima might just be right about talking to a photograph—after all, in ancient times people must have had a reason for drawing on the walls of their caves the prey that they were hoping to run into when they went hunting. If they'd had glossy magazines back then, the Cro-Magnons probably wouldn't have daubed soot on stone walls with charred sticks, they'd simply have cut out photos of bison and mammoths and jabbed their spears at them during their magical rituals ... so she might as well try to work a bit of magic with a photo—but surreptitiously, so her friends wouldn't laugh at her.

"Hey, Misha Botvinik," Lena thought to herself. "Can you hear me? You know what women are like nowadays, don't you? Of course you do. Well then, I'm not like that. Honestly, I'm not … I'm … well, you can't even imagine what I'm like. I'll do the very best thing for you that one creature can do for another. The very, very best thing. Can you hear me? I swear!"

The minibus braked, the magazine jerked in Lena's hands, and she thought she saw Botvinik wink at her briefly with his left eye. Then she started feeling stupid, turned over half the pages in the magazine in one go, and came to the section on low-budget eligible bachelors.

There were ten of them on each page, and to be quite honest, they weren't very inspiring. The photos were passport format, with strange recommendations printed under them in small type, for instance: "Rapidsher Verbitsky, GQ's mathematician of the year." Lena glanced at Rapidsher, sighed, closed the magazine, and put it down quickly on an empty seat—in order not to confuse matters.

•

Once, when Lena watched a German film about Hitler's final days, the thing that struck her most forcibly of all was how nondescript the entrance to the Führer's underground bunker looked—she couldn't understand why anyone would make so much fuss over something so dismal.

The route to her new workplace turned out to pass through an equally inconspicuous concrete structure, like the shelter at a bus stop or the entrance to a public toilet. And furthermore, this entrance was located on a military base, behind a barbed wire fence, with armed soldiers standing all around.

Nor was she impressed by the elegance of the elevator in which they found themselves after their documents were checked. It was a simple iron cage with a ribbed floor—though it was very spacious. And when they reached the bottom (after riding down for ages), her mood was completely ruined.

Everything was exactly like in the film about Hitler. Concrete corridors with low ceilings, cables strung along the walls, iron doors, vents, hatchways, cold fluorescent lighting. However, the air was fresh; it even had a kind of forest fragrance.

The girls were taken to a dressing room with several metal cupboards and a shower, and told to wait.

A few minutes later, Uncle Pete entered the room with the major, who collected their signatures on a nondisclosure agreement. The major was still wearing his camouflage uniform and Uncle Pete was in a jaunty t-shirt with a slogan that read:

HUGO BO⚡⚡

Lena spotted the Nazi runes, but she didn't get the point at first.

"That's because Hugo Boss designed the SS uniform," Kima whispered.

"Sounds about right for a place like this," Lena whispered back.

"No talking in the ranks!" the major barked.

When they stopped talking, Uncle Pete said:

"All right, girls, today is just an introductory day—there won't be any clients. Presently we are in your dressing room. This is where you'll get changed. Then you will proceed along the corridor, through the metal detector, to the place where you'll be working. The dressing room is located in the technical zone of this complex and there's a cafeteria nearby where you can always purchase refreshments. Now for the specifics. You are the Caryatids of the Malachite Hall. Which means that before your shift, you will smear yourselves with malachite paste. It's absolutely harmless—a tinting cream developed especially for you. And you have wigs—they're lying over there. The wigs can be put on before the injection, a special opening has been left at the back.... Right, what are we gawking at, my little daisies? Let's get naked and smeared up!"

Lena didn't find the procedure difficult, she had long ago accustomed herself to the idea that on the path to success she would often have to undress in front of strangers. Although the "malachite paste" was repulsive gunk—it looked like green, pearly shampoo—on the skin it turned into a fine, glossy film with a pattern that really did resemble a polished slab of malachite.

"Rub it on thoroughly," said Uncle Pete. "On the eyelids too, because you'll be standing with your eyes closed."

"Does it let the skin breathe?" asked Asya.

"Yeah, sure it does," Uncle Pete replied. "And by the way, next time your mound has to be shaved, just remember...."

Asya blushed, but she didn't say anything

When she finished smearing herself, Lena pulled a wig of green dreadlocks onto her head. The dreadlocks were woven out of something like bast fibres and gathered together into a pharaoh-like hairstyle. The wig was large and luxuriant, yet so light that she could hardly even feel it on her head.

"All right girls, down on your knees," said the major, and the familiar injection gun appeared in his hand. "Let's pretend we're at Katyn. Don't worry," he snickered, "it doesn't hurt."

And it really didn't.

The injection felt like a cool fountain suddenly spurting at full power into the back of Lena's head. (Lena thought she had experienced this feeling before, either in her childhood or in a dream). The fountain struck her brain, bathing it in a cold stream that washed away the seething mass of anxieties and thoughts that Lena hadn't noticed until they revealed themselves by disappearing.

It was strange. After the injection nothing drastic occurred. It simply became clear that before it Lena had been in a state of extreme agitation—a kind of fidgety, frightened panic for which there was no reason except that it was her usual condition. But as soon as this internal commotion passed off and tranquillity descended, the nervous trembling of her body, which Lena hadn't noticed before either, came to a halt. Everything became calm and very clear.

When Lena looked at herself in the mirror, she was dumbfounded.

Gazing out at her from the gleaming rectangle was a stone idol. Those were the first words that came to her mind.

Of course, there was no comparison with the crude, weathered carvings of the Siberian steppe—this idol was made of polished malachite, and its hair seemed to be carved, rather coarsely, out of the same material. Only its eyes were still alive. Lena tried closing them and looking at herself through her eyelashes. That made the similarity to a statue complete.

Lena held her hand out in front of her and looked at her green fingers. They were absolutely unfaltering. It looked as if any one of them would break off if it was tapped with a hammer, and the others would carry on jutting out into the air in the same motionless way for thousands and thousands of years.

•

The Malachite Hall turned out to be a large square room faced with malachite and decorated with frescoes on spiritual subjects. Uncle Pete explained that it was a free adaptation of one of the halls in the Hermitage, the empress's former reception room.

There was no furniture in the room apart from a huge sofa shaped like a bagel. Standing in the empty center of this sofa was a retractable table—a round slab of malachite on a hefty telescopic leg that ran down through the floor. The sofa was upholstered in brightly patterned silk, with numerous cushions of various colors and shapes scattered about on it. On the table, crystal and glass sparkled and glinted green.

In each corner of the hall there was a malachite base or pedestal. Above each of them was a prop for the Caryatids' hands (they were supposed to support the ceiling), and the height of the props could be adjusted by a special mechanism so that when little Aysa and tall Vera climbed up onto their pedestals, they could assume exactly the same pose, with their arms raised to meet the upper malachite slab at exactly the same angle. In this pose their elbows pointed forward, exposing their armpits, which they had to shave thoroughly before every shift.

No normal person could possibly have stood motionless in that pose all day long—but after the injection it wasn't a problem. Lena's body seemed like a light glass flask, with some invisible flame of life burning inside it. She knew that an external observer would only notice this flame when she opened her eyes. According to their instructions, they could only open their eyes when they were talking to a client, but Lena had already realized that she could observe her surroundings through her eyelashes and no one would ever know.

However, there was absolutely nothing to observe.

During their first shift on the job the hall didn't have a single visitor. A few times she heard rollicking, drunken voices and laughter from the corridor outside the entrance. And once she caught the smell of a Cuban cigar, which reminded her of Uncle Pete.

During the two days she stood on the pedestal, Lena was able to study every last detail of the hall.

The frescoes showed levitating, long-haired angels, dressed in identical white robes with strange-looking watermarks. The angels hovered above a strip of cloud, holding each other's hands, and seemed to be listening to something quiet. However, the religious theme was not too intrusive. First, the angels were indulgent—that much was clear from their smiles. And second, their eyes were covered by black blindfolds. Even the bearded God the Father wore an identical blindfold. (The inconspicuous door of the staff entrance, through which Lena and her friends had arrived at their workplace, was located in His stomach.) God the Father had His hands raised, but He seemed to be spreading them in protest, as if to say: "Don't ask for anything more, guys. I've already given you everything I could."

Evidently the intended meaning was that God is not exactly what the simple, common man is told—and He's not particularly bothered by the frolics of the elite, whom He Himself has exalted to the pinnacles of power.

It was rather strange to see clouds one thousand feet underground, but Lena was well aware that the heaven where God and the angels lived was not a physical space: everyone knew that Gagarin and Khrushchev had had a serious falling-out on that score.

Every few hours the table sank under the floor with a quiet hum and a few moments later rose back up into the hall, freshly laid. It was set with liquor, wine, champagne in an ice bucket, hors d'oeuvres, and fruit. And although no one came into the room during the first shift, the table traveled down and up again eight times—and every time the refreshments on it were replenished.

Lena felt as if she had been standing on the pedestal for almost no time at all. Her mind was working in a special kind of way, unusually light and precise, and she was planning to think about a lot more things, when the door in God the Father's stomach opened and four green female figures entered the hall. They were the new shift—apparently the two days were already over.

•

"Did you see him?" Asya asked before the following shift.

"Who?" asked Lena, puzzled.

"The praying mantis."

At first, Lena thought that Asya meant the praying angel on the main door—he was located opposite the service door in God the Father. But then she recalled the insect from which the Mantis-B serum was made.

"No," she answered. "I didn't see him. Where?"

Asya shrugged.

"I don't know. Inside."

"Inside yourself?"

"I suppose so," Asya answered, giving her a mysterious glance. "Or maybe inside the mantis."

Lena thought Asya was fooling around.

However in the middle of the next shift something very odd happened. Lena suddenly felt as if her hands were not raised upwards, but folded in prayer in front of her.

Or rather, it was the other way around. It felt as if for a long, long time, almost from the very beginning of time itself, she had been holding her hands folded in front of her chest, and then she had had the illusion that they were raised above her head and pressed against a slab of stone. And then she realized that the illusion she had had was her real situation. And then it was like when you wake up in the morning and it becomes clear that this absurdly squalid and unconvincing continuation of your dream really is the truth, and now you have to get up, get dressed, and go out into the world to feed yourself.

Lena thought she must have dozed off while she was working, and she felt frightened, because she could fall off the pedestal if that happened. But when the hallucination was repeated, she realized that it had nothing at all to do with sleep. This time she followed exactly what was happening much more closely.

She was in two places simultaneously. One place was the Malachite Hall. It was hard to say anything definite about the other space, which was flooded with blinding sunlight. It quivered and shimmered like the picture in a kaleidoscope, stretched by some unusual optics to span a full 360 degrees, but a kaleidoscope would have been uninteresting compared to what Lena saw. If her surroundings could be compared to anything, it was the visuals that Windows Media Player created when it played MP3s. Even though this space was so bizarre, Lena took a liking to it immediately, because she experienced its waves of multicolored lights as happiness, which kept changing color and shape but never ceased to be happiness and never got boring.

There were two Lenas. One was standing on a malachite pedestal in the corner of an empty subterranean hall, with her hands pressed against a block of stone over her head. The other was bathed in a stream of living sunlight, holding her hands folded in front of her chest. They were unusual hands, with lots of sharp little fingers sticking out at right angles, like nails protruding from a plank. The sharp points of the fingers pricked her palms pleasantly, encouraging a feeling of self-confidence.

There was no contradiction between the two Lenas. But there was one big difference between them. In the place where Lena was human, she was a false stone idol, working a long shift in one of the auxiliary spaces of an underground brothel. But in the place where Lena was a praying mantis, she was ... well, that was where she was a real person. At least that was the way she would have liked to put it.

It felt as impossible to express all the thoughts that flooded through her as it was to explain exactly what it was that the Windows Media Player drew. But one thing was clear—after glimpsing that strange, sunny world, it was sad to return to the *Sextine Chapel* (as Kima had dubbed the Malachite Hall after their first turn on duty)—even taking into account the immense competition for a place as a Singing Caryatid and the unreal amount of money that was paid for the job.

Lena was so engrossed in all these thoughts and feelings, she didn't notice that that no one came into the Malachite Hall during her second shift either. This time there weren't even any voices in the corridor or cigar smoke.

•

After their shift the girls went for a bite to eat in the staff cafeteria, located at the end of the corridor that passed by the dressing room. The cafeteria was the only underground area that their passes gave them access to—the corridor had many more side branches, but they were closed off by turnstiles that didn't respond to a magnetic card with the words "Malachite Hall" on it. (Lena didn't actually try to get in anywhere, she believed what curious Kima told her.)

The cafeteria had a festive look, but the cheery atmosphere was rather somber somehow—the place was reminiscent of a military mess hall that someone had decided to convert into a disco. The walls were decorated with cheerful cartoon film graphics and brief texts rendered in two colors—red and blue. Red was used for various everyday aphorisms, and blue for definitions of beauty (the idea here was probably to prevent the staff from getting too laid-back and to keep them constantly measuring themselves against a high standard).

The posters in red looked like this:

*THE SUPREME SIGNIFICANCE OF RUSSIAN LIFE IS
THE CALM, PATIENT GILDING
OF A BOUNDLESS ICONOSTASIS*

*IN THE FUTURE EVERY SNAIL
WILL REACH THE SUMMIT OF MT. FUJI
FOR FIFTEEN SECONDS*

*SOVEREIGN DEMOCRACY
IS BOURGEOIS ELECTORAL DEMOCRACY
AT THE STAGE OF DEVELOPMENT
WHEN DEMOCRACY IS STILL DEMOCRACY,
BUT THEY CAN EASILY F.. K YOU UP THE A..S
IF THEY WANT TO*

The blue maxims about beauty were mostly quotations from newsmakers of years gone by:

"BEAUTY WILL SAVE THE WORLD."
– FYODOR DOSTOEVSKY

"BEAUTY SUCKS D..K."
– LARRY FLYNT

*"BEAUTY IS THAT ELUSIVE QUALITY,
ALMOST INEXPRESSIBLE IN WORDS,
THAT ALLOWS A WOMAN TO BE A BITCH FOR A
WHILE BEFORE THEY CART HER OFF
TO THE GARBAGE DUMP."*
– KATE MOSS

When she saw the word "dick" written with dots, Lena wanted to ask Kima if that was counterculture, but she felt too shy. Kima doubted that Larry Flynt and Kate Moss had ever really said anything like that, but she agreed that basically there was nothing objectionable here.

Hanging in the corner of the cafeteria was a Soviet-style wall newspaper with underground news and drawings by the staff—it was predictably called "Kthulhu and the Bear Are Listening!" and its masthead was a skinny, lilac octopus with spectacles drawn onto it so that it looked like a bald Lenin. As the line filed past, Lena tried to read what Kthulhu was thinking about. The octopus's thoughts proved to be rather misanthropic and sometimes downright insulting. Lena was particularly horrified by this:

The fundamental quality that a modern Moscow girl cultivates by the age of twenty is the naive readiness for elite hyperconsumption (in today's Russian this is known as "pussyness"). Any fool knows that no one is going to let these legions of pussycats anywhere near a glamorous sugar daddy, he'll simply mess with their heads and then dump them. Basically, that's the way it's always been, throughout history. But today the means you have to use to mess with a girl's head are so crass that the reward awaiting you for this dirty, heavy work pales into insignificance. Especially since these efforts not only offend the moral feelings of a decent, Christian human being, but are also extremely expensive—and the true market price of the anticipated reward is significantly less than the bill for the first dinner in a good restaurant. And discussing the possibility of spiritual affinity with one of these Prada-wearing amoebas would simply be a waste of time ...

Then Lena read another article that explained the word "electoral" from the sovereignty poster:

To call the Russian public an "electorate" is approximately the same as calling passive sexual victims in prisons "pederasts" ("lovers of boys" in Greek). What can we say? Yes, this term is indeed widely employed, consecrated by custom, and it is actually possible to find certain factual grounds for such usage. But even so, there are moments when it is hard to rid yourself of the feeling that behind this grandiloquent foreign word lurks a sinister grin, not to say a malicious lie ...

At first Lena had read "electoral" as "electro-oral," and it was only when she finished this passage that she realized that what was meant was the exact opposite.

"So people aren't unhappy with just one thing," she thought wearily, "they badmouth everything about our lives. Why don't they just leave the country? ..."

The wall newspaper's frankly critical attitude to the established order of things was astonishing—but Kima shrewdly explained that it was deliberate, to give the cafeteria's patrons a feeling of complete, elite access to anything and everything.

"A pocket dissident," she said, "is something like an evil dwarf jester in cap and bells. In glamorous circles it's actually regarded as rather chic to be one."

Lena thought Kima must be right, because for some reason no one in the line really lingered too long over Kthulhu's secret mouthpiece.

The cafeteria was crowded. People in technical uniforms made up most of the crowd, but there were colleagues of Lena's too: standing in front of her were several young Atlantes in skimpy loincloths. They must have worked in some kind of classical interior, because their sculpturally defined, muscular bodies were smeared with a marble-like powder. The powder had been rubbed off the buttocks of one of them, and he had a clear handprint on his thigh. The others kept looking at him and grinning.

The feeble small talk the girls were making gradually fizzled out. And then out of the blue Asya asked: "Did you all see it?"

"What do you mean?" asked Lena, puzzled.

"The praying mantis."

Lena nodded. Vera and Kima just glanced at each other, which made it clear that they had seen it too.

"I think I was praying," said Asya.

"Because of the way your hands were folded?" asked Lena.

"Not only that. It's just a prayerful kind of state. All the worldly voices inside you quiet down and there's nothing left except unity with a higher reality. That's what prayer is. That's what my granny taught me when she was still alive."

"I didn't notice a special unity with anything higher," said Vera. "It was certainly calm, though. And simple."

"That *is* unity," said Asya.

Vera chuckled.

"Higher, lower, who can tell the difference? But did you see the pipe under your feet."

"I don't see any pipe," said Asya. "I think it's the branch the mantis is sitting on. And it gives me a headache, because it's in front of me and behind me and right up close all at the same time."

"That's the way a praying mantis's eyes are arranged," said Kima. "It sees everything on all sides. So the branch really is in front of you and behind you."

"And what kind of mantis is it?" asked Vera. "Where is it?"

Kima thought for a moment and said:

"It's the archetypal praying mantis. Comprehensive and universal. The mommy and daddy of all praying mantises who have ever been and will be. It exists in Platonic space."

"And what does it do there?"

"It prays," said Asya. "I'm absolutely certain about that."

Three Mermaids came into the cafeteria: Lena had seen one of them outside the Radisson-Slavyanskaya Hotel— she recognized the mole on her cheek. The Mermaids had taken off their tails and were dressed in short, scaly t-shirts that glinted under their bathrobes, with swimming caps on their heads. Lena studied them for a while with a mixed feeling of envy (all three of them were miraculously beautiful) and superiority (Lena definitely wouldn't have wanted wet work like that). The Mermaids kept looking at the Caryatids too, but soon got fed up with trying to stare them down, and the girls went back to their interrupted conversation.

"Maybe we should tell Uncle Pete everything?" Lena suggested.

"No way," replied Vera. "There'll be investigations, and all sorts of commissions of inquiry.... They'll start looking for side effects and close down the hall. Are you tired of being paid, or what?"

No one had any answer to that.

Other colleagues arrived in the cafeteria. Two golden-haired kids with toy bows got in line behind the Mermaids. They were escorted by a hirsute man with silicone breasts, draped in a mantle of purple linen cloth. He had a very clear, broad love bite on his neck. Vera sized up the new customers with a sideways glance.

"Everybody's got work already," she said, "we're the only ones left ... like brides without bridegrooms."

Kima giggled.

"I asked the girls from the last shift if they'd had anyone there or not. At first they said they'd signed an agreement and told me to get lost. But then one of them, Nadka, said there had been three men who looked like government officials—they just dropped in for a few minutes. The girls took a fix on their age and started singing 'Another Brick in the Wall.' But the guys didn't even look at them—they just drank a bit of vodka, ate a few mushrooms, and left."

"And have the other girls seen the praying mantis too?"

"I think so," said Kima. "Only they don't want to talk about it…. Lena, stop daydreaming. Take your plate and get up to the cash register, or the Mermaids will push their way in."

•

On their next shift Lena got an answer to her question—she learned that the mantis could see her too.

Contact occurred during the fourth spread from the start of the shift (a "spread" was what the girls called the time interval between every resetting of the round table). At that moment Lena was gazing absentmindedly through her eyelashes at one of the angels on the wall (the folds of his robes hinted at an erection, which in principle shouldn't happen to a sexless being, even in a place like this).

It all started the same way as the last time—Lena suddenly saw her hands folded in front of her chest. And then a strange, triangular head appeared in front of her—it reminded her of a comic-strip alien. There were two large, faceted eyes set on the sides of the head, with three smaller eyes set between them. And all five eyes were gazing at Lena. The mantis also had very serious jaws. But Lena wasn't frightened.

"???"

The mantis spoke to her somehow without using words, but Lena understood everything.

"I work here," she replied. "I'm waiting for clients."

"???"

Lena realized that she too could answer without words, simply by lifting a kind of screen in her mind and letting what was behind it spill out and become accessible to the mantis. So that was what she did.

"----"

The mantis did the same—it removed the barrier separating its consciousness from Lena's, and something absolutely incredible flooded into her.

It could be described approximately as follows: whereas the last time Lena thought that the world around her had turned into something like the visualizer in Windows Media Player, now she herself became the visualizer, and the world disintegrated into a host of discrete aspects that taken separately seemed absurd, astounding, impossible, and terrifying, but together somehow balanced each other out in a calm and happy equilibrium that settled into her head.

This equilibrium permeated everything. For instance, Lena still didn't know who it was in front of her—an individual mantis or the spirit of all mantises. But that didn't matter at all, because if it was a spirit she was looking at, it lived in every mantis, and if it was a simple mantis, the spirit spoke through it. The two possibilities were simply opposite poles of what was actually happening.

In exactly the same way, it was not clear what happened

at the moment when their minds fused—whether she became the praying mantis, or the mantis became her. But that didn't matter either, because the being that arose between these conceptual opposites couldn't care less who had become whom.

The mantis didn't ask itself questions like this. It didn't think in terms of words or images at all. It simply was. It was a drop in an infinite river that flowed from one vastness to another. Every drop in this river was equivalent to the entire river as a whole, and so the mantis had no concerns about anything. It knew all about the river, or rather, the river of life knew all about itself. It flowed through the praying mantis which, by becoming Lena, had allowed her to catch a brief glimpse of this miracle forgotten by man.

The miracle also consisted of a balance of opposites. It could be said, for instance, that the mantis knew everything—insofar as its five eyes even saw the beginning of the world and its end (Lena was afraid to look in that direction, it made her feel too dizzy). But it could also be said that the mantis didn't know anything, and that would also have been the simple truth, since it really didn't know anything itself—infinity was simply reflected in it, as the whole world is reflected in a drop of water. In fact, she could have guessed all this without the praying mantis, there had been a time in her childhood (or even before that) when she knew it—but now this self-evident thing had been forgotten, because the daily itineraries followed by the adult mind were located on an entirely different plane. But here, with the praying mantis, it was impossible not to remember it.

Lena was so enthralled by all these experiences that she stopped being aware of where she really was.

Now she knew why the praying mantis had five eyes. The small eyes set on the front of its head, between the feelers, saw the past, the present, and the future—that was why there were three of them. And the two big faceted eyes on the sides of the head were simply appendages to the eye that saw the present—they perceived its form and color (the past and the future didn't have these qualities, but the mind extrapolated them). It was such a simple and rational arrangement, Lena felt surprised that everything was so different in human beings.

The eye of the mantis that was directed toward the past saw the black abyss of nonexistence (it wasn't black, and it wasn't an abyss—but that was how it was reflected in consciousness). The eye directed toward the present saw the Malachite Hall with its four green caryatids. And the eye directed toward the future saw Uncle Pete.

He was wearing a red t-shirt that Lena hadn't seen before. It said "DKNY," decoded as "Divine Koran Nourishes You."

·

Uncle Pete really did come to the meeting in a t-shirt with the four letters on it:

DKNY

That proved that during the last shift, Lena really had seen the future. Only the future had changed somewhat in the meantime: Uncle Pete's t-shirt was blue, not red, and the decryption under the four-letter code was different— "Definitely Kthulhu, not Yahweh."

Uncle's Pete's face was red, though.

Everything became clear once he started to speak.

"Yesterday," he said in the voice of a newscaster announcing the start of a war, "at eleven forty-two in the evening, an act of terrorism was averted in our complex. Averted at the very last moment. Ekaterina Simoniuk— born 1990 and employed as an erotic decorative element in the blue billiard room—attempted to blow herself up. Shortly before that she had had plastic surgery. In fact the operation was plastic in more than one sense—instead of silicone Ms. Simoniuk had modified gelatiniform plastic explosives, produced in Pakistan, implanted in her breasts. She intended to detonate the charge using a device disguised as a lipstick. This attempted terrorist act occurred when two Category A clients were playing billiards. If the guards had not shot her ..."

Uncle Pete squeezed his eyes shut and ran one hand over his bald cranium. Lena noticed that although his head still seemed to be smeared with cigar ash, there were more white flecks in the ash than dark ones; just recently he had acquired more grey hairs.

"In the blue billiard room," Uncle Pete continued in a calmer tone of voice, "the billiard table stands on six legs that give blowjobs. Kind of like sphinxes with swan's wings—its a pretty complicated makeup job. Ekaterina Simoniuk was one of these legs. Before the terrorist act she tried to shout out the Shahadah in Arabic, but thank God, a member of the security service responded immediately by shooting to kill. He has been recommended for a decoration. The potential victims of the terrorist attack did not even have time to realize what was going on, they thought the girl was just trying to attract attention.... We're checking her contacts now, following up the Chechen connection—we have information that the suicide bomber was from the Riyad-us-Saliheen Brigade, although she is not Chechen by nationality. As they say, Basayev is dead, but his cause lives on.... Girls, I understand that all this has nothing to do with you, but this incident will have serious consequences for all of us. An ideologist is going to start working with you. Don't worry, not some Soviet-style old fart. A normal, modern young guy who'll explain everything to you in human terms so you don't develop any metastases in your brains...."

"We won't get metastases there anyway," said Vera. "Unless those injections trigger them, of course."

Uncle Pete didn't dignify that remark with a reply.

"And now about our work," he said. "We're doing a lousy job, girls. Oh, yes. In all this time there have only been three client-shows. And not a single one during your shift. If things carry on like this, we'll have to say good-bye to the Malachite group. And we'll schedule the hall for replanning. Make it the Mowgli room, or a little nook with a Tadjik girl for extreme snuff. Murmurings are already being heard among the shareholders. That's just so you know."

"You're saying we'll get sacked?" asked Vera.

Uncle Pete put on an offended expression.

"Well what do you think, kiddo?" he replied. "Our top national priority is a competitive edge on the market. Lose your competitive edge, and you're out. No one's going to feed us for free."

"But how is that our fault?" asked Asya. "We do everything we're supposed to. We're prepared to be competitive. You're the ones who have to bring in the punters. Maybe you could spread the word a bit wider, about this wonderful Malachite Hall …"

"What does that mean, 'spread the word?' Information doesn't get spread the way you think. Only by word of mouth. Someone looks in, likes it, and he tells someone else. Has anyone looked into your hall? They have. But they haven't brought anyone else."

"Probably it's the religious frescoes that put them off," said Lena. "Maybe they feel ashamed in an interior like that.…"

Uncle Pete gestured impatiently.

"Don't talk nonsense," he said. "The frescos develop the theme of the Malachite Hall in the Hermitage.… Although God only knows, I suppose you could be right—what do you think they ought to paint on the walls?"

"Ask the artist Kulik to do it," Lena said, surprising even

herself. "Let him think of something."

Most of what she knew about Kulik was what she'd heard from the culturally sophisticated Kima, and she was afraid Uncle Pete might ask some trick question that would expose her ignorance. But he just jotted something down in his notebook.

It's not only the pictures that are to blame," Asya put in. "Clients walk along the corridor without even glancing in, I've seen it. Maybe they simply don't know that we're alive? We stand there completely still. And we stay silent."

"Now, that's more like it," said Uncle Pete. "You stay silent. But what kind of Caryatids are you? Singing Caryatids. So why the silence? For your pay you can sing too."

The girls exchanged glances.

"Are we going to sing all the time, then?" asked Lena.

"What's wrong with that?" Uncle Pete chuckled. "Songs, my little sweetheart. Music by composers."

•

After careful thought they decided not to include songs in the continuous program. It required too much concentration from the performers, and also, in Uncle Pete's opinion, the words of the songs could disrupt the clients' leisure by engaging their attention and undermining their comfort. It was decided that initially the performance would be limited to a "polyphonic purr," as Kima put it— and they would only move on to the song repertoire at the client's request.

They included two types of purr in the program. The

first was the theme from *Swan Lake*—they got that down quite quickly. The second purr was based on the song "Mondo Bongo" from the film *Mr. and Mrs. Smith*. All they left of the lyrics, which referred inappropriately to the CIA, was a "la-la-la-la-la-la" that looped back on itself like a feather-light paper streamer, before collapsing altogether into a kind of shamelessly sweet delight. The resulting jingle could be purred in four voices, without stopping, for the whole forty-eight-hour shift—it was a beautiful and economical solution, in the sense of economy of effort.

During the first musical shift, when they were fine-tuning "Mondo Bongo" (they sang two at a time, each pair for an hour), there were still no visitors. But this time there was a legitimate reason: the artist Kulik was at work in the Malachite Hall—Uncle Pete had commissioned a new mural from him after all.

The most interesting thing was that they never saw Kulik himself—his assistants did the work, and it was done incredibly quickly: they finished the entire job in one day. First the young guys in yellow boilersuits covered the sky and the angels with an even layer of cream undercoating. Then they switched on a slide projector and traced the outline of the image projected onto the wall: the result was a rather crude human shadow with disproportionately long legs, framed by the words "woof!" "WOOF WOOF!!" and "WOOF, WOOF, WOOF!!!" written in all sorts of various fonts—from wacky comic to gloomy gothic. These various-caliber "woofs" covered the entire wall, overlapping each other, and the guys in the boilersuits filled them in with different colors, checking against charts laid out on the floor. It all turned out very beautiful and interesting, like some sort of bright Central Asian ornamental design—only in Lena's view, it was all spoiled by that dark shadow wearing some kind of hat or cap. It wasn't clear what all this was supposed to mean until the artists painted a verse epigraph in an upper corner of the wall and the name of the composition in a bottom corner. The epigraph was this:

A breathless night. Dogs in the distance
Cleave the stillness with motley barking.
....
We enter—my shadow and I.
Sebastopol, April 1919

The composition was called "Nabokov in the Crimea."

Uncle Pete examined the mural with mild skepticism and inquired what Kulik's own personal contribution was going to be, if the work was already finished. The senior assistant, a young man who looked like Hermes, with a beard woven into a braid, explained condescendingly that this was only the preparatory stage, the most important part was still to come: determining between which two walls a chain could be stretched, so that the master could be attached to it.

Uncle Pete frowned when he heard that.

"What for?" he asked.

"He's going to move along the chain on a special collar ring, with a dog skin thrown across his shoulders, and masturbate over a little plastic figure of a schoolgirl clutched in his hand. And once he's sexually aroused, he'll spontaneously fling himself on your clients. Like Caligula in *The Lives of the Twelve Caesars*."

"What kind of skin?" asked Uncle Pete, staggered.

"A dog skin," the assistant repeated. "But if you want to camp it up, by all means, we can order a bearskin. Or even a nostalgic old black Labrador—if you can get it approved. We've already got a special grant for the black Lab—we'll be doing that later in Frankfurt—but there's no publicity for your installation, am I right? So we can do it. It'll be absolutely unforgettable. Just imagine it, eh? Your guests will live with that energy for the rest of their lives...."

Uncle Pete led the assistant out into the corridor.

Since they didn't put up the chain, Lena concluded that the artistic conception had been successfully simplified.

While the artists were working and coming to an understanding with Uncle Pete, Lena underwent several new and very unusual experiences.

Just like before, she felt that she was holding her hands folded in front of her chest. But now this feeling was joined by another phantom sensation—she felt that she had a second pair of legs supporting her long, long, very long body. Lena knew that this was a hallucination, since the second pair of legs would have had to be far behind the wall, and that wasn't possible according to the laws of physics. But the feeling was far more real than any of those laws.

During one of the breaks when the artists went out for a smoke, and Lena didn't have to sing, the praying mantis briefly reappeared And just like the previous time, the exchange of information between them was wordless and virtually instantaneous.

Lena explained that what she was doing with her mouth was music, useful work for which other people fed her, because of its beauty. The mantis informed her that mantises had a completely different kind of music—one note that had been sounding for millions of years without changing. Lena expressed curiosity as to how one note could be music, if it never changed. It doesn't need to change, the mantis transmitted back. What makes it beautiful is that it will always be like that, no matter what happens. Lena wanted to hear that eternal note, but the mantis told her that she heard it anyway, she simply didn't take any notice of it. Then Lena inquired if they could speak to each other in words, and the mantis answered something between "we'll see" and "some other time."

This entire dialogue took no longer than a second.

And then, as if he could sense what Lena really wanted, the mantis again revealed his incredible, clear, and eternally unchanging mind to her. After that there was no point in talking, and Lena gazed spellbound at the shimmering mother-of-pearl eternity until the end of her shift.

After work Lena always felt shattered. The journey back into Moscow was especially hard for her—that was when the effects of the Mantis-B finally wore off. Every time Lena began to feel depressed—the human world to which she had to return seemed like such an uncomfortable place. *Counterculture* helped—she had gotten used to reading it on the return journey, curled up into a bundle of suffering by the window of the minibus. (Asya, who sat beside her, preferred the Orthodox Church glossy magazine *Lust of the Eyes* or the business weekly *The Pride of Life*, which the driver always bought.)

As she read, Lena worked her way back into a reality that lashed at her errant consciousness with its trenchant, savage lines:

> The victory at Eurovision will not be the last! The country is learning to play by the world's rules and making ever more serious investments in cultural expansion. According to information agencies, work is going on in Russia to create a fifth-generation queer by subjecting Boris Moiseev to fundamental modernization using nanotechnologies. Experts claim that this new Russian development will substantially surpass the closest western equivalent—Elton John. In this connection, observers remark that some fifth-generation technologies (for instance a total hair transplant) are still beyond the reach of Russian specialists, but believe that they can compensate for this backwardness by using augmented botox injections.

The serious intellectual effort required to understand some of the information helped Lena to recover her equilibrium.

In his *Tractatus Logico-Philosophicus*, Wittgenstein claimed to have discovered a general form for the description of all sentences in any language. In his opinion, this universal formula includes within itself every possible semiotic structure—just as the infinite space of the universe includes every possible cosmic object.

"That there is a general form," Wittgenstein writes, "is proved by the fact that there cannot be a proposition whose form could not have been foreseen (i.e. constructed). The general form of proposition is: 'such and such is the case' ('Es verhält sich so und so')."

However the philologist Alexander Sirind, an associate professor at the Irkutsk Teacher Training College, successfully refuted the famous formula recently when he adduced the example of a proposition that transcends the Austrian philosopher's all-embracing paradigm. It sounds like this: "Fuck off, Wittgenstein."

"The Austrian made the mistake of forgetting old man Schopenhauer," says the academic, "but after all, the world is not just idea, it is also will!"

Practically all the information that Lena came across was imbued with self-assured pride in the country's success. Everything was permeated with it now—even the weather forecast and the blurbs on books—and that made the world outside her window a little more comfortable.

In his autobiographical dilogy *Black Earth* and *Downfall into Brooklyn*, the Moscow correspondent of *Time* magazine, Andrew Shmaier, investigates the cultural and psychological shift taking place in the Russian consciousness, as a result of which a poorly paid western journalist (in former times the object of girls' dreams and an almighty figure with the attributes of a deity) loses his attractiveness as a potential sexual partner and, in the eyes of the compradorist Moscow elite, is transformed into a banal cocktail reception parasite, who is dreary and depressing to talk to and absolutely good for nothing.

However, she was finally brought down to Earth by an advertisement aimed, as always, at recognition of the image it had already created:

"Free Space." I'll get a wash and go to the mountains! ™

Even this relatively smooth reentry mechanism did not provide complete protection. A few journeys like this were enough to make Lena to realize that human reality does not consist of time and space, but of various whisperings, mutterings, outcries, and other voices. She didn't know who they belonged to. Some resembled her parents' voices, some were like her friends', but the words spoken by them were wreathed in oppressive meanings that were vague but absolutely inescapable—for instance, a voice sounding like Kima's repeated a strange phrase over and over again: "the glossy analysis of romantic stubble with which the countercultural heroes tickle the Fabergé Egg system." Lena wanted to ask Kima what it was the heroes tickled with—the romantic stubble or the glossy analysis —but she realized the question would sound strange.

When the praying mantis went away, these voices

started chattering hysterically in her mind, clamoring for her attention and tossing it to each other by turns, until soon they became so frequent and dense that they overlapped each other, forming something like a basin that someone had put over her head.

After that, she didn't see the world as it really is (that was where the praying mantis lived), but only the interior of this basin—the human dimension. She knew the same thing was happening to her friends. It was obvious from their faces.

At home, Lena locked herself in her room and waited for four human days to pass by until she could ride out of Moscow again to spend a little time with the praying mantis. For that she was willing to sing the purr from "Mondo Bongo" and the mix from Tchaikovsky and the anthem of the USSR in English (that was Uncle Pete's latest commission)— basically she would do anything at all.

The world of mantises was a good place to be. There was no gloom in it—that is, if you didn't count the need to return to the Profsoyuznaya metro station in a minibus with a placard that said "semiotic signs." But in the world of people everything was … not exactly totally unbearable. It was just that … Lena had trouble finding the right words, until one day Asya offered her thoughts on the subject.

"It's kind of like guided dreaming with Nadezhda Pravdina," said Lena. "We learn to dream about shit, because that means money's on the way."

"If we recall that life is a dream," Kima replied from her seat by the window of the minibus, "then we get the formula of modern civilization and culture."

Such indeed was the case.

•

Uncle Pete arranged the promised meeting with the ideologist as a picnic with campfires and shish kebabs on the bank of a canal. A lot of people came to the lecture—three busloads of guys and girls. Most of the faces were unfamiliar. Lena recognized the young Atlantes she had seen in the cafeteria, the Caryatid Varya from the third shift, one Mermaid, and the hirsute man with the silicone breasts, dressed in a shapeless smock instead of a purple bedspread. He was conspicuously drunk and kept sipping from a flat flask that he took out of his pocket.

Lena had a short conversation with Varya, whom she had only met once before at the introductory session in the Slavyanskaya Hotel. Varya had a big bruise under her eye, thickly smeared with pancake makeup. Apparently there had been a combined corporate function and birthday party in the Malachite Hall two days earlier. The entire company was celebrating—some kind of "special service venture yids" as Varya described them vaguely and incorrectly. They had brought several crates of French champagne with them, and ten of their own broads.

"Would you believe it?" she complained. "These guys fired the champagne corks at us! And not just them, they set their little whores on us too, and they laughed and kept aiming for our faces, from just six feet away. You try singing 'Happy Birthday' with that going on. They broke Tanya's nose and almost put my eye out. If I could get my hands on those bitches, I'd kill them on the spot...."

"Did you finish the song?" Lena asked sympathetically.

"Yes," Varya replied, casting a meaningful glance at the man with the silicone breasts who was listening to their conversation. "What else could we do? Why's that man with tits eavesdropping on us?"

Lena wanted to talk a bit more, but Varya said she had to finish reading the book she'd brought with her—the other girls in her shift were all waiting to read it. The book was in English and it was called *Singing in Awkward Positions: The All-Inclusive Manual by Eros Blandini*. Eros Blandini, Vera explained, was a castrated dwarf who worked as the sound effects for the magical fairground attraction "The Singing Head." He had spent his long life singing out of lockers, crates, and dark corners while lying, sitting, and even standing on his head.

"Why are you reading it?" asked Lena.

"Oh, come on!" said Varya. "It's got all the technical moves in it. There's this rule—if you want to stay in business, even just stay where you already are, you have to keep growing all the time, because other people are trying to grow too and sideline you."

Lena felt a strange pang—not exactly envy, not exactly jealousy, not exactly fear. She didn't say anything, just wrote down the title of the book so she could tell Kima about it, because she knew English.

The ideologist arrived very late.

He got there after dark, when the shish kebabs had already been eaten and the campfires had burned out (they had to be lit again). He was a man about forty years old with pleasant, regular features, like the faces they used to draw on Soviet posters. Everyone was surprised to see him dressed in a full Second World War uniform, including a helmet and waterproof cloak, but the ideologist explained that he'd come from a rehearsal for another function and hadn't had any time to change. He got straight down to business without any delay.

"You had an explosion," he said, taking off his helmet. "Well, you almost did, it's the same thing. The most important thing now is to feel our way into the psychology of this failed terrorist and understand why Ekaterina Simoniuk wanted to inflict such a tragedy upon you. She doesn't appear to have had any reasons for hatred. In her job she earned more in a month than both her parents do in a year. Why did she try to commit this act? Let's think about this question for a minute or two."

While everyone was thinking, the ideologist took off his groundsheet cloak, exposing a soldier's tunic worn outside his trousers.

"Now let me tell you what I think about this. As everyone knows, before she died, Ekaterina Simoniuk tried to shout the Shahadah, and the security forces are working on the Riyad-us-Saliheen Brigade theory at the moment. But the Chechen terrorist connection here is only secondary. I'll explain why...."

The ideologist ruffled up his hair several times, as if he was trying to electrify his head. It seemed to work—he frowned and started talking quickly.

"The Shahadah is an Arabic oath pronounced in order to declare a person's acceptance of Islam. To understand why a Moscow girl born in Ukraine accepted this religion, we must ask ourselves the question: What is modern Islam? According to its leading political theorists, it is a religion of the oppressed. Yes indeed, my friends, of the oppressed. So why, then, did Ekaterina Simoniuk, with her astronomical salary, feel like an oppressed victim in our city? After all, she could indulge herself far more freely than her friends or her parents from Kharkov, let alone her parents' parents. So why did this girl join the ranks of the Black Widows? That's the real crux of the matter. Does anyone understand why?"

The man with the breasts muttered something and everyone stared at him. But he didn't say anything else.

"Then I'll try to answer this question. You are all familiar, boys and girls, with the doctrine of the Invisible Hand of the Market, which sets everything in its right place by redirecting people and resources to where there is an effective demand. Our life today seems to be arranged like that. But the doctrine of the Invisible Hand proceeds on the assumption that a human being is a rational creature who always makes decisions based on an understanding of his own advantage. The pioneers of the nineties who laid the foundations of our present prosperity—admittedly, with mistakes and excesses—held precisely this view of human nature. But it has all turned out to be far more complicated. The human being is not arranged in the way the economists thought. He or she is motivated by irrational as well as rational factors. Have any of you heard of the so-called ultimatum game?"

There wasn't anybody on the grass who had.

"It's a well-known economic experiment to study the motives of human choice. The essential point is simple. You and the person you are playing with are given a certain sum of money. The other person decides at his own discretion how to divide the money between the two of you, and you can accept his decision or reject it. If you accept it, each of you gets the amount that your partner decided on. If you don't accept it, no one gets anything at all. Got that?"

"Yes," said voices from out of a darkness with orange sparks flying over it.

"Now this is where the most interesting part starts. The ideal *homo economicus*, as the theory describes him, should accept any decision made by his partner in the game. After all, even if he is only given one percent, he's getting money for nothing. And if he rejects his partner's decision, he misses out completely. But research indicates that most people prefer to end up with nothing if they are offered less than thirty percent of the total sum. It's irrational. But that's the way the human brain works."

"I'd take fifteen percent," a voice called out.

"And I'd take whatever I was given," said another voice, "and then I'd come back at night and kill them all."

"Thank you for those opinions," the ideologist replied. "But please let me finish. In actual fact it's much more complicated than that. One secret economics institute in Moscow conducted special research on the ultimatum game, in which an important amendment was made to the standard form of the experiment. The player who had to accept or reject the decision about dividing up the money was shown a photograph, instead of another live player, and then told how that person had apportioned the money. So, they showed the players photographs … "

The ideologist frowned as if he had suddenly recalled something unpleasant.

"We won't name any names," he continued, "you already know the top rankings on the Forbes list. Well then, in this case there was a significant deviation from the standard threshold of 70/30. For some reason with these people our fellow citizens would only agree to equal shares.

"Like Sharikov in *Heart of a Dog*," an ingratiating voice said out of the darkness. "Divide everything up."

"I'm not sure that's a good example," the ideologist responded. "Let's not discuss why we have this slide toward a 50/50 threshold. There are many reasons, and they must be sought in our complicated history and culture, in our communal psychology and national character. What is important is to remember that these attitudes exist in our minds, and our enemies are learning to exploit them. That's why they brainwash us by constantly rotating photographs of various Russian oligarchs like Abramovich and Prokhorov in the mass media and describing their freakish whims and revels. What they're counting on here is very simple—to provoke in the common man the same feeling that makes the player in the economic ultimatum game give way to a furious desire to restore justice and lose everything in the process. But while in a laboratory experiment, this decision remains no more than a statistic, in real life its results can be tragic."

The ideologist stopped speaking, as if to give everyone a chance to appreciate the full weight of what he had said. Silence descended on the canal bank.

"Is it hard to take part in the ultimatum game and maintain a rational outlook? Of course it is. But that, boys and girls, is precisely why we must regard ourselves as warriors—oh yes indeed, warriors on the psychological front. Only very recently, one of your sisters-in-arms, Ekaterina Simoniuk, played her own version of the ultimatum game with destiny. And she lost everything, including her own young life. I'm certain that if she was sitting at this campfire with us now, she would be struck, as we all are, by the thought of how important it is to maintain a cool, sober state of mind. All of us—I say 'us' because this is my problem too—need to learn to move beyond the irrational, unconscious impulse that destroyed Ekaterina Simoniuk. Do not be envious. Today's Bentley driver is tomorrow's cop on the beat, heh-heh...."

"It's the other way around," a cheerful young voice shouted from the fire, "today's cop on the beat is tomorrow's Bentley driver!"

"That happens too," the ideologist agreed amicably. "But so what? That's the way life is. To see all this and hold firm—that, if you like, is our own Orthodox jihad. In the genuine, spiritual sense of the word ..."

He coughed to clear his throat as if embarrassed at such exalted and inspired words, and continued in an ordinary, everyday tone of voice.

"Basically, we have to keep in mind the most important thing, boys and girls. In the modern world there are powerful forces that aspire to exploit our natural human irrationality for their own purposes. And they are often successful. I'm sure that this is what happened in the case of Ekaterina Simoniuk. This tragedy shows just how much impact the media bombardment from London and New York actually has on our minds. Don't think that you are too smart or above all this. Don't think that the brainwashing doesn't work on you, that it's some kind of foam plastic seventeen point two. The brainwashing even works on me. The only thing we can do is learn to keep our emotions under control. Just remember this: in the age of political technologies, sooner or later our most natural and spontaneous feelings are mobilized in the mercenary interests of others—there are entire teams of professional scoundrels working on that. There is an undeclared war going on, and every time we feel in our hearts a pang of apparently just resentment at the excesses of our wealthy Russian knuckleheads, the oligarchs of London rub their sweaty hands together and laugh...."

"That's really clever," Lena thought respectfully, "twisting everything around like that, just like a Möbius strip. I'd never have thought of anything like that. Very smart."

For some reason the lecture had a counterproductive effect on the silicone-breasted man who was sitting beside Lena. In him, the flame that was supposed to expire flared up instead. He finished off the indeterminate liquid in his flask and started muttering, gradually raising his voice:

"Fancy fucking thinkers ... One's worked on the documents, another's worked out the numbers. And they've all got firm handshakes, the bastards. But we'll still be sucking dick underground, the same as ever...."

"You mean you have clients?" asked Lena.

The man raised his eyes to look at her.

"Sure," he replied. "Why, don't you?"

Lena didn't say anything.

"Where are you from?" the man asked.

"The Malachite Hall," Lena replied proudly.

"What do you do there?"

"We sing there. Colored to match."

"The Malachite Hall...." the man muttered. He already seemed out of his mind. "They'll drink their champagne, and we'll sing for them, colored to match. And not only sing, we'll actually fight for the right to sing to them. Compete against each other ... fucking architects. And how did it all begin, eh? A lack of social justice, that's how. The fucking Politburo built itself a great big dacha...."

The ideologist listened tensely to this voice of the people and attempted to ride the storm. "That's right!" he said, raising one finger. "And now, for fuck's sake, there's not enough freedom for them. It's the same thing happening again, not a micron's difference. They're pushing the same program. And they want to screw us according to the same schedule."

"Get lost, you jerk," the breasted man whined. "Fuck off, you scumbag...."

The ideologist took offense.

"Then perhaps you'll continue the lecture?" he said. "Since the two of us seem to be giving it together."

But the breasted man had already lost interest in external reality—he started hiccupping violently, so they dragged him further away from the fire just to be on the safe side.

After the lecture Lena wanted to approach the ideologist, but there were too many people around the fire where he was standing. Primeval red shadows played across the ideologist's face, and that made his answers seem especially weighty.

"Just think for yourselves, boys and girls—this Kasparov, who needs him? It's like us sending some Yakut to

New York in a t-shirt that says, 'Brooklyn, Wake Up!'"

"But he's the champion of the world," someone said uncertainly in the darkness.

"And exactly what is a chess champion?" asked the ideologist, turning toward the voice. "He's not a prisoner of conscience or some kind of social thinker. He's something like a man with a very big dick. Only Kasparov hasn't got it up for years, if you check the tournament tables. Maybe Eduard Limonov is interested in this business for old times' sake, but what's it to us? No, boys and girls, the age of political pygmies working for Pindostan is gone forever. Finished. They can sing a final song of farewell, if they like...."

Lena realized that the spiel about Kasparov's big dick, which brought a flash of enthusiasm from the gathering, was not part of the prepared lecture but an association that had occurred spontaneously to the speaker. As he finished his talk and said good-bye, the ideologist got dressed in something extremely strange. Instead of his tunic, he pulled on a tight-fitting sleeveless rubber garment that ended in a hood with a nipple. A small opening had been cut in the hood for his face, and the garment itself was colored like the Russian flag.

A black Lexus was already waiting for the ideologist. Squeezing himself into the back seat with an inelegant but energetic jerk of his entire body, he shouted a final "So long!" through the window and drove off into the night, dropping long sparks out of the window from the cigarette that the driver had put in his mouth.

"They've given him a job at the ministry," Varya explained. "A nice, cozy spot. But the rest of the mob's getting the push. They're preparing for their farewell event, a youth protest called 'No to Spiritual AIDS.' Fifty thousand dickheads on Lenin Prospect."

Then Varya whispered in her ear that Ekaterina Simoniuk hadn't died the way their bosses had said. She wasn't planning to blow anyone up, she just gave too much lip to some big-time Caucasian types who were playing in the blue billiard room.

"She just lambasted them from under the table. 'We don't want all you wild animals here,' she said. 'Go on back to your mountain village, the white mule can give you a blowjob.' Well, that got them really riled—who likes to hear things like that, when they've paid good money, and they're high on cocaine? They prodded her with a cue and it got her in the eye. It happened by accident, no one meant to kill her. The PR people invented all that stuff about plastic explosives and the Shahadah. There are heaps of them on the staff, but there's no work—this is a classified project. So they're trying real hard. But at least the lecture was interesting, wasn't it?"

•

The visitors entered the Hall of the Singing Caryatids at the tail end of the final spread, when Lena and her girlfriends were wearily purring their way toward the end of the theme from *Swan Lake*.

There were four of them—a short, fat man in a shaggy robe, two guards in expensive double-breasted suits, and Uncle Pete in a t-shirt that said:

D&G
discourse and glamour

From the abject way Uncle Pete fussed over the fat man, Lena realized he must be someone very important. And then she recognized exactly who it was.

This was incredible....

It was Mikhail Botvinik standing down there, looking exactly like in the photograph that she had spoken to in the minibus—with the same bright blush covering his entire face and the same part in his sparse black hair.

Lena almost fell off her pedestal. So Kima had been telling the truth! Of course, in theory Botvinik could have just dropped in of his own accord—but no power on earth would ever convince Lena of that.

Botvinik jerked his chin upwards in a distinctive gesture that she had seen before on television.

"What are they singing?" he asked.

"Tchaikovsky," Uncle Pete replied. "Incredibly beautiful music—we took a long time choosing it. Sounds like it's about some primeval mystery, doesn't it?"

"Ha," said Botvinik. "You know which mystery that is? That Tchaikovsky lived with his own coachman. The coachman was the husband, and Tchaikovsky was the wife. He even took that coachman to Italy with him. There's your primeval mystery for you, six hundred and eighteen, trunks, my precious trunks."

"You think that's what the music's about?" asked Uncle Pete, startled.

"Of course," Botvinik replied. "being determines consciousness. Ta-ti-ta-ti ta-ta.... That's the sweet, melting feeling he got when his coachman stuck it up him...."

Lena saw Kima, who was standing opposite her, take her hand off the marble slab and show her two fingers. That was a secret sign. Lena repeated the same gesture for Asya, because she couldn't see Kima. A few seconds later all four of them started purring "Mondo Bongo" in perfect synchronization.

"Whoa," said Botvinik, impressed. "How do they do that?"

"They took note of your criticism," Uncle Pete said with a smile. "And switched to a different composition. You can dance to it with any of the girls, if you like."

"I'm not some kind of queer, to go shaking my ass about," Botvinik said and nodded at Lena. "Is she jabbing those two fingers at me?"

"No," answered Uncle Pete. "They're coordinating the change of music."

"How d'you mean?"

"Okay now, Lena," Uncle Pete said with a wink, "go back to Tchaikovsky...."

Lean gave the sign to Kima, and she passed it on to Vera, who couldn't see Lena, and the girls switched back smoothly to *Swan Lake*.

"Not bad," Botvinik laughed. "I'll have to bring the guys around."

He pulled in his stomach, tightened the belt of his robe, and winked at Lena.

"Stay cheerful, Greeny. I'll definitely pay you a visit. I'm just a little beat right now, after the Mermaids…."

As he spoke, Botvinik took a yellow plastic rhomboid out of the pocket of his robe and dropped it on the floor. Uncle Pete raised one eyebrow, but didn't say anything, and followed Botvinik and his bodyguards to the door. A minute later he came back on his own, picked up the yellow rhomboid, kissed it, and said:

"Girls, this is a chip from our casino. Twenty-five thousand bucks. Five thousand for each of you and a commission for me. Now do you see where you're working?"

When Uncle Pete left, the praying mantis appeared to Lena and asked:

"????"

"It's money," Lena explained. "There isn't anything like that yet at your stage of development."

"????"

"That's the oligarch Botvinik," Lena replied. "He's got lots and lots of money."

"!!!!"

Lena sensed that the mantis thought Botvinik was a threat. To understand what the matter was, she had to open the door in her mind again, and the mantis's strange feelings filled her consciousness.

This time she learned a lot that was new.

Apparently, near the very end of its life, a praying mantis started to fly (this was nature's way of making its old age interesting). During its flight, it was sometimes attacked by a sinister black shadow that tried to swallow it. There was nothing terrifying about this; on the contrary, for some reason that Lena didn't yet understand, to die like that seemed like a blessing. But the rules of life required the mantis to fight for existence and dodge the bats, by randomly changing its direction of flight. That was why the mantis had a hollow cavity in its body—a kind of resonance chamber, a special "ear of darkness." Its function was to spot the approach of danger from a distance. And right now that ear sensed a threat.

Lena finally understood.

"Silly you," she said. "It's not a real bat. It's just a tattoo on his shoulder. Besides, you couldn't have seen it, he was wearing a robe. How do you know about it?"

From the answer, Lena realized that the mantis had seen the tattoo in the magazine photograph—it had been imprinted on her memory. But the problem wasn't the tattoo, the problem was that the ear of darkness had heard darkness. It was very hard to understand exactly what the mantis meant and what it wanted. Its wordless feelings passed straight through Lena's consciousness like a rippling rainbow and disappeared.

"Can you say it in words?" Lena asked, frustrated.

"Yes," the mantis suddenly said in a human voice. "Only they'll be your words, not mine. But if you like, I can speak with your words and thoughts."

The mantis had a baritone voice that sounded both confident and confidential at the same time, a voice borrowed from a FM radio announcer Lena often listened to. Lena guessed that the mantis had found this voice in her memory too.

Only they didn't get a chance to talk—the shift was over.

•

The next time Botvinik brought his "guys," as he had promised. There were three of them, apart from him, all wearing fluffy bathrobes, and to judge from their flushed faces and wet hair, they had just been through some kind of hydrotherapeutic procedure. They brought a deck of cards and paper to write on.

One visitor made quite a serious impression on Lena. Unlike the others, he didn't have bare legs sticking out from under his robe, but general's trousers with a broad red stripe. But it wasn't just the stripes. He reminded her somehow of the major in the blotchy camouflage suit who gave them their injections before the shift—but he didn't simply have the same kind of face; he seemed to represent an extreme development of that human type (if you locked fifty hungry and ferocious majors in a dark basement and opened the door a week later to let out the only survivor, and then raised him to the rank of general for the next twenty years, you'd get something like this man). But strangely enough, beside Botvinik's flushed features, that scary face seemed childishly defenseless.

The other two had a dejected air—one was a sturdy guy with a beard, who looked like a sectarian engineer, and the other one kept turning his curved back toward Lena before she could get a good look at him. Both of them behaved fawningly—they were probably petty subordinates of some kind.

If Botvinik remembered Lena at all, he didn't show it.

After removing the hors d'oeuvres and drinks from the table, the visitors settled down on the circular divan and started playing Preference. Soon one of them asked for the "muzak" to be turned off, and until the end of the shift Lena and her friends enjoyed the forgotten delight of idle silence, broken only by the voices of the players.

Lena listened to the conversation. It was about something strange.

Gradually she began to understand that the visitors were discussing the Combat NLP technology that had been such a total mystery to the author of the article in *Eligible Bachelors of Russia*.

"I'm trying to polish up the seventh form," the general announced. "First alignment and control, then disruption of the stereotype, then elision and apposition, right?"

"Right," Botvinik agreed.

"But last time, Misha, you said the seventh form had to include complete disruption of the stereotype. What does 'complete' mean?"

"There's also partial disruption, General."

"But what's the difference?"

"A theoretical explanation would be too long and complicated. Let me give you a specific example. Complete disruption is, for instance, 'Go suck your fucking mother's dick.' And partial disruption would be, 'Go suck an old rabbit's dick.' But note that 'Go suck a retired groundhog's dick' is complete disruption of the stereotype again. Get it?"

"What's so hard to get?" the general said with a sinister chuckle. "But tell me, Misha—does it have to be elision first and then apposition? Or can it be the other way around?"

"However it comes out," said Botvinik. "Don't get too hung up on the theory, Comrade General. Combat NLP is a practical skill. Above all, keep trying it on the punching bag. Feel out the sensitive points."

The general turned to the stocky man with a beard.

"Hear that, old Fartov! Shall we practice a bit?"

"I'm not old Fartov, Comrade General," the man replied morosely. "My name's Perov."

"Prickov-Dickov! Before you go correcting your elders, take it out of your ass, you dumb chickenshit. Open that beak again and I'll wallop your bald-headed dick so hard, there'll be nothing left but the cock-a-doodle-doo, and they'll find your dick behind the wardrobe, you fucking mongrel's condom. Whose brains do you think you're rinsing your dick in, you fucking marketologist? Do you know how many of your kind have died on my dick?"

"Offensive words, Comrade General," the bearded man responded, looking indifferently through his cards. "Cruel and unjust. What kind of marketologist am I? I'm an expert."

"Well, how was it?" the general asked, turning to Botvinik.

"Definitely C-grade. The alignment was fine, but then you ran off the tracks."

The general frowned.

"Hang on, Misha," he said. "There's something I'm not getting here. Did I rupture his stereotype or didn't I?"

"Of course not," Botvinik replied. "You never even got to that. You're not rupturing his stereotype, you're putting him in a negative double bind."

"A double bind?" the general exclaimed in surprise. "That's when there are two contradictory suggestions, right? But where?"

"You told him, 'Take it out of your ass.' So just think like he would for a moment. If he takes it out of his ass, you'll be asking for him from the escort company in five minutes' time. So he's got an internal conflict. He's got no time to worry about stereotypes."

"So how do I get out of it?"

Botvinik thought for a moment.

"Remove the threat. Restore hope. Let's say, instead of just 'Cock-a-doodle-doo', give him 'A quiet cock-a-doodle-doo for *Escort* magazine.' Only you have to make sure the dick behind the wardrobe comes at least eight hundred milliseconds after the information packet with the cock-a-doodle-doo, so the prefrontal cortex has already had time to process that. Don't talk so fast. Then we can get by all right."

The general scratched his chin thoughtfully.

"But that bit about finding his dick behind the wardrobe," Botvinik continued in a different tone of voice, warm and slightly ingratiating, "was very competent and subtle, Comrade General. I'd even call it talented, for Christ's sake. Because here we have complete disruption of the stereotype on the subconscious level."

"Why on the subconscious level?" the general asked, frowning again.

"It's obvious. Think for yourself. How does his dick get behind the wardrobe? Only from out of the subconscious. The client hasn't had enough time to comprehend anything yet, and there you have a breach like the gash in the side of the Titanic. And then you throw two more pricks in through the breach to reinforce the impact, so there's no way he can ever slip off the hook. I couldn't have thought that up myself. It has the style of a real strategist. A military head is a military head, true enough."

The general cleared his throat benevolently.

"Do you always analyze everything that deeply?"

"I don't analyze any longer," Botvinik replied. "It's all intuitive. You gradually develop this kind of clear channel of maximum effectiveness that you can sail along without even thinking. It comes with experience."

"I should note that down on the flowchart," said the general.

Botvinik waved his cards

"Forget about flowcharts! They'll be no use when you're attacking someone for real. What is Combat NLP? It's spontaneity, direct sensory impact. As my sensei used to say, it should leave the smell of burnt feathers. There was a time I used to work from the head too—I used to think, I'll disrupt the stereotype, and then the job's almost done. But that's intelligentsia-style thinking. You have to work from the heart and rupture his asshole, not his stereotype. This method works when you apply it constantly, unconsciously, like breathing...."

These philological novelties were too complicated for Lena, and she soon stopped following the conversation. Then she saw the praying mantis again.

First her hands seemed to be folded together in front of her chest, as usual, and then the triangular head appeared in the air. It was closer now than before, and Lena noticed yellowish spots of light glittering in the mantis's central eyes. She finally realized what those three eyes had been reminding her of all this time—they were arranged like the circular blades of her father's electric razor.

"What are those yellow lights?" she asked. "That shining?"

"That's the truth," the mantis replied in the same voice it had started using the last time. "If you have questions, you can ask the lights and you'll see everything."

Lena pondered. She had no more serious questions about life left—everything had been clear for a long time. Only rhetorical questions came to mind.

"Why is everything here arranged like this?" she asked.

The answer immediately appeared in the mantis's eyes.

It was startling—the way the swirling patches of light and spots of color formed into something like a short cartoon film with a very clear meaning. This meaning wasn't directly connected with the picture, but somehow it found its way through to her consciousness.

Lena saw something like a bloody cherry pit. The pit was gradually covered by flesh, then skin, and then it was covered by tufts of white fluff. Incredibly beautiful crystalline snowflakes started appearing on the ends of the tufts—but by that time the strange fruit on which they were growing had completely rotted away, and the snowflakes showered down into the darkness with a sad tinkling sound.

"Do you understand the meaning?" the praying mantis asked.

"I do," Lena replied. "Here, everything new and good always starts with some detestable crime. And when this new, good thing yields fruit, the detestable crime yields fruit too and the result is that everything gets jumbled up together and dies. It's something premeval, sad, and inevitable—it's always been that way here and it always will be. But what's going to happen to the snowflakes?"

When the mantis showed her, Lena had to take several deep breaths to pull herself together.

"But do we have to go there?" she asked pitifully. "Can't we go somewhere else?"

The patches of light in the mantis's eyes went out.

"Where do you want to go?" he asked.

"Remember, you showed me, right at the beginning," Lena replied. "That place … how can I put it … that flowing stillness. I can see in all directions at once, and there's such peace in everything, and I don't feel afraid of anything anymore."

"You're talking about the world of praying mantises," said the mantis. "Are you sure you want to go there?"

"Of course," Lena whispered.

"To become a praying mantis, you have to pass an exam. Then you can be born and die in our world as many times as you like."

"What kind of exam?"

"You'll have to transgress the bounds of human morals," the mantis replied.

"Well, that's no problem," said Lena. "We're used to that. What do I have to do?"

"Next time," said the mantis and disappeared.

The end of the shift was gradually approaching.

The card players who had stayed for so long cursed loudly every time the table with the cards and the score sheet disappeared under the floor and then reemerged covered in fruity splendor again. Even Perov the punching bag demonstrated his mastery of Combat NLP—he went down on all fours beside the hole in the floor and yelled into it.

"Lousy queers! Don't touch the cards! I'll kill you fuckers if you mix the cards up again!"

But this time around Botvinik didn't even glance at Lena.

•

The major in the dappled uniform stood in the corner of the dressing room, winding up the ribbon of ampoules again, pretending he was counting them for the second time. Lena had long suspected that he deliberately came into the dressing room half an hour before the injection in order to watch her and the other girls getting changed.

The injection gun was sticking out of the waist of the major's camouflage trousers, and Lena found herself contemplating certain extremely unpleasant associations suggested by that. If not for Uncle Pete, who had also unexpectedly come to inspect his troops, she would have insisted on the injection gun being washed with soap, but she didn't want to start a squabble in front of the boss.

Uncle Pete was in an excellent mood—he was smoking a cigar, dropping the ash on a black t-shirt that said:

CCI General Directorate

"Girls," he said when the major had loaded the injection gun, "an announcement. Today Lena has an exclusive client, Mikhail Botvinik."

Though Lena had been expecting to hear this, she suddenly felt nervous and dropped the jar of malachite cream on the bench.

"Supposedly he'd just flown off to London," Uncle Pete continued, "and suddenly decided to come back. So you must have sung well, Lena. Or kept silent well, I don't know. He phoned—he'll be here in two hours."

"I won't go," Lena said and burst into tears.

Uncle Pete didn't even pretend to take that seriously.

"What's all this, Lena," he drawled lazily, "have you totally flipped? You'll earn enough to pay for half an apartment in a single stroke. And you'll earn your Uncle Pete here enough for a quarter of a dacha plot. Stop playing the silly girl. All things are good in moderation."

"That's right, Lena," said Vera, pulling the green lamp shade of a wig onto her head—I would have thought you would be jumping for joy, way up to the ceiling. But instead you throw a sulking fit. I'd scratch your eyes out for a client like that, honest."

However, Lena had already come to her senses.

"Okay," she said. "I don't have to sing, right?"

"You don't," replied Uncle Pete, "but the other girls have to pull out all the stops. Vera, you're in charge of the music today. Let's have something lyrical instead of that purring. Or you can choose something yourself. Have you calmed down?"

That question was meant for Lena.

"Yes," she answered. "Can I have two injections today? Just to make certain."

"Make certain of what?" Uncle Pete asked and giggled.

Lena shrugged and put on a cool expression.

Uncle Pete looked at the major.

"I sign for every ampoule," said the major. "By number and date. You can sign for it if you want."

"I'll sign, what's the problem?" Uncle Pete agreed. "You can see the girl's nervous. What if Botvinik suddenly asks her to stand like a praying mantis and she can't do it? Just to avoid any slipups, heh-heh …"

While the first injection had always felt to Lena like a cool fountain spraying into the back of her head, the second one was like a gust of arctic wind that instantly transformed all the water in the fountain into little crystals of ice. Lena knew right away that she now had a second pair of legs and an ear of darkness. The sensation was very clear, and she had to concentrate all her willpower to convince herself that it was only the usual somatic hallucination that followed the injection.

"Girls," she said, hiding her second pair of legs behind the first, "Just don't look when Botvinik comes, all right?"

"All right," Asya answered for all of them and smiled approvingly.

The praying mantis appeared in front of her soon after she climbed up on the pedestal and set her hands against the upper block of malachite. This time Lena could see his head far more distinctly than usual. She noticed little notches in the antennae that protruded from the region of the central eyes. And now the real world—the Malachite Hall and her friends standing on their pedestals—seemed blurred and approximate.

The mantis got right down to business, as if their previous conversation had never been interrupted.

"In order to become one of us," he said, "you'll have to do this…."

And its three central eyes showed Lena a cartoon film that was appalling but absolutely clear, while the two big faceted eyes watched her reactions closely.

Lena had been prepared for anything at all, but not this.

Now she realized what the mantis had meant when it talked about transgressing the bounds of human morality. It turned out that it hadn't been exaggerating at all.

"Never," said Lena.

"I'm not coercing you," the mantis replied.

"No," Lena repeated in horror. "I'll never be able to do that."

"It's one of the laws of the world of praying mantises."

"Do you even understand what you just suggested?" asked Lena. "It's absolutely beastly."

"It's not beastly," the mantis replied solemnly. "It's insectly. We've been doing it for almost half a billion years. And not just praying mantises, either."

"Who else?"

The mantis's head moved so close that it almost touched her, and its big faceted eyes looked deep into her soul.

"For instance, *Pisaura mirabilis*. During the nursery web spider's amorous intercourse, the female eats a fly caught for her by the male. And the female *Oecanthus niveux* sucks the juice out of a special gland in the male tree cricket's body. The female *Lystrocteisa myrmex* eats food regurgitated by the male jumping spider straight out of his mouth— which, by the way, is how your human kiss developed, though two hundred million years later. Only people, as usual, have done away with the substantial part and left just the PR. Praying mantises simply take the most radical approach to the problem...."

"How do you know all these Latin words?" asked Lena.

"It's not me, it's you. All this is what you know."

"I've never heard anything of the kind."

"Once, by chance, you happened to run your eyes over an article on this subject," said the mantis, "and your brain remembered it all. You're just not aware that you know it. That kind of thing could never happen to a mantis."

Suddenly the mantis disappeared, as if something had frightened him away.

And the next moment Lena saw Mikhail Botvinik entering the Malachite Hall.

•

Botvinik was accompanied by his two usual bodyguards in double-breasted suits and Uncle Pete, who had found time to change into a black t-shirt that said:

ADIHIT

Below the inscription was the Adidas triangle, split into its trademark bands—but only two instead of the usual three, which made the triangle look like Hitler's toothbrush moustache.

The bodyguards stayed over by the doors while Botvinik and Uncle Pete walked into the hall.

Botvinik was trying to prove a point to Uncle Pete, continuing the conversation started outside:

" ... that's why I say the fresco's faggoty. Pure faggot. He wrote about it in his poems. I don't remember exactly where, I was young when I read it. For instance, he has this poem where he screws a little Greek boy, like Lord Byron. And then slits him with his knife ... with this superhuman Nietzschian laughter ..."

"Where's that part?" asked Uncle Pete.

"Now, how does it go?" Botvinik muttered, frowning as he tried to remember. "'And then I laugh, and suddenly the beloved Anapaest flies off my pen....' Actually, Anapaest's the only faggot here, you can't really charge the author with anything. But from certain other little verses you can. He wasn't interested in young girls, he was just pretending so people wouldn't realize who he really was: five-eighteen, there's a jackdaw flying past ... The nobles had a distinctive code of honor too."

"I don't know," said Uncle Pete. "When it comes to poetry, I prefer Esenin."

"And what do you like him for?"

"For his style," answered Uncle Pete. "'You are my Chardonnay, my Chardonnay ...' Divine."

Botvinik crossed himself and spat.

"Know what Oscar Wilde said? Style is the last refuge of the faggot."

"Probably," Uncle Pete agreed timidly. "So did Lord Byron really ... you know, with his little Greeklings ... Greek kids?"

"What do you think?" replied Botvinik. "He even kept a diary. Okay, I'm not some lecturer from the Knowledge Society."

He glanced around the room and spotted Lena.

"Hi there, Greeny!" he said with a smile. "See, I came—just like I promised. I've got half an hour."

Behind Botvinik's back, Uncle Pete made wild eyes, swinging his chin downwards. Lena realized that meant she should get down off her pedestal. She tried to do this as gracefully as possible, jumping down onto the floor, absorbing the impact with her knees, and sinking into a courteous but highly dignified curtsey.

"Well, you're a great gymnast, Greeny," Botvinik murmured.

"I'll be going then," said Uncle Pete, "you can sort things out here for yourselves. Music, girls!"

He walked to the door. Vera started singing "The Wheels of Love" and Asya and Kima purred along, imitating the instrumental accompaniment—it was a number they'd put together a long time ago, with Lena singing the second voice part. She wasn't singing now, but even without her it sounded pretty good.

Botvinik took off his robe, leaving him in just his shorts—black boxers, exactly what the last Russian macho ought to wear. Lena saw the tattoo on his shoulder, the famous bat.

Then the praying mantis returned.

Of course, Botvinik didn't notice anything. Lena had already figured out that she could talk to the mantis right in front of Botvinik and he would never know. And what's more, her communication with the mantis took place at such great speed that she and the mantis had already discussed quite a lot of things in the time it took Botvinik to walk over and take her by the hand. The mantis moved its head close to her, and its three central eyes played a rerun of the animated film showing what she had to do.

It didn't seem so terrible to Lena now.

"But why the head?" she asked.

"It's a general law of the universe," the mantis replied. "The eating of the male always begins with tearing off the head by any means available. As if you didn't know, heh-heh, it's what all your women's magazines train you to do. And it affects sex, from the physiological point of view. When the braking mechanisms are removed, the amplitude of spasmodic reflex movements is maximalized. For instance, if you block a frog's higher nerve centers, it spontaneously makes frictive copulative movements Tearing off the head is a metaphor, which is realized quite literally in the world of mantises…."

"Where did you learn to talk like that?" Lena asked. "For

instance, how do you know the word 'metaphor'?"

"I've already explained that once before," replied the mantis. "You're the one who knows all these words—I merely use them."

"But I don't understand even half of what you say," said Lena. "It definitely didn't come out of my head."

"Have you got a computer?" asked the mantis.

"Yes," said Lena.

"What do you think, would you recognize all the pictures you can find with it?"

"Of course not."

"This is the same thing. Don't get distracted. Make up your mind quickly."

Lena sensed that she really did have to make up her mind now: Botvinik was already leading her over to the sofa.

"I'd like to ask the girls' advice," she told the mantis, but then realized she was asking the impossible.

However, strangely enough, the impossible turned out to be possible: all three of her friends instantly appeared in her lower field of vision—like interpreters on TV, translating into three different sign languages. Vera was singing about the wheels of love, Kima was purring the accompaniment, and Asya was looking straight at Lena, only moving her lips for the sake of appearances.

"Asya," Lena called to her, "can you talk?"

Asya nodded.

"Do you know what he wants me to do?" asked Lena. "I mean the mantis, not Botvinik."

Asya nodded again.

"He's been working on me too, since the first time we met."

"But why didn't you say anything?"

Asya lowered her eyes guiltily.

"I thought I was the only one with that kind of craziness in my head. I was ashamed, because it seems really bizarre. But when I got home, I looked in the encyclopedia and read that it was true. The female praying mantis really does eat the male immediately after … you know what. She tears his head off and eats him."

Lena turned to Vera.

"I didn't know at first either," said Vera. "But then I looked it up in the internet. She does eat him, it's true. Entomologists even joke about it, they say it's obvious why the mantis prays. He's praying for the forgiveness of his sins."

It was strange how, even while she was talking to Lena, Vera kept singing "The Wheels of Love." Perhaps this conversation with her friends was just a hallucination, but anyway, the moment Lena thought about that, the girls disappeared from her field of vision and the question ceased to be relevant.

Especially since there were only three steps left to the sofa.

The praying mantis appeared in front of Lena again.

"Well?"

"I don't know," Lena said and burst into tears.

But she was only crying in the dimension in which she communed with the mantis. Where she was walking toward the sofa with Botvinik, probably only a fraction of a second had gone by.

"What's bothering you?" asked the mantis. "Why are you crying?"

"I promised to do the very best thing possible for him."

"For who?" asked the mantis.

"For Botvinik in the photograph. That's why he came to me. But this is so cruel …"

"You think it's cruel?"

"What else can you call it?"

The mantis became sad. Lena sensed that he would go away forever now, and there would be nothing left in the world but the divan drawing closer and closer, and an old song by Nautilus Pompilius.

"Wait," she said. "There must be something I don't understand. Maybe you can explain?"

"Look into my eyes," said the mantis.

Lena saw the short cartoon film again.

She was looking at something like a meadow flooded with sunlight—a blinding, trembling, shimmering space, distorted (or perhaps rectified) by the insect's faceted eyes. There were two praying mantises sitting in this meadow, but Lena understood that this was a pure formality. What she was actually seeing before her was the endless river of life with which she was already familiar, flowing through the mantises, through the sun in the sky, and through her as well.

This river did not rest on anything, it was absolutely free and not constrained by anything. It existed in and of itself. And yet in some way its existence was contingent upon the praying mantises and Lena.

She suddenly realized quite clearly that all living things—flowers, insects, birds, animals, and even people—didn't just exist for themselves, for no particular reason, but for one single, solitary purpose: to provide a channel for this great river. All living things *were* this channel. But at the same time they were also the river which, in some mysterious and inexpressible way, flowed through itself, unlike the way earthly rivers flowed.

Lena saw the channel being constructed. It all happened right in front of her eyes: two praying mantises united with each other to initiate new life. And when the sacrament was completed, one of them did the very best thing that it could for the other—by setting it free. And then the part of the great river that had been flowing through that mantis was liberated and began flowing through itself, and this was the greatest possible happiness. Lena had no more doubts about that now.

"I understand," she whispered. "Now I understand. So it's not cruel at all, quite the opposite?"

"Cruelty," the mantis replied, "is keeping someone here for too long. To be alive is to dig the channel. To depart is to become the river that flows along it."

"But why don't any people know about this?" asked Lena. "I have to go back and tell everyone!"

"In the first place," the mantis replied soberly, "anyone who wants to know will find out without you. And in the second place, it's better *not* to tell everyone you meet about it. That's a bad thing to do. Stupid and absurd."

"Why?"

"Surely you can see why? Because the great river knows what it is without you. But sometimes, for a little while, it wants to be a prostitute, or a cat, or a geranium in a vase. Or even take a peek into a place like your city. So why should you explain to it what it really is? You'll ruin all the fun of the outing."

"I understand," whispered Lena. "So praying mantises simply help each other to go back home. And this is the very best thing that one creature can do for another? Exactly what I promised?"

"Of course," the mantis said in a soulful voice. "That's the reason why our lovemaking ends in this noble gesture. The female does it for the male, because he has fulfilled his duty, and from now on he is free. Naturally, the male would be glad to do the same for the female, but she still has to care for their offspring."

That sounded convincing.

"I won't have the strength to do it."

"Yes you will. I'll help."

Just then Lena and Botvinik finally reached the divan.

Botvinik sat her down on the soft silk, and at that moment the praying mantis Lena had been talking to disappeared, but Lena noticed that Botvinik himself had become a mantis.

He was ash-colored, with a narrow little head and expressionless faceted eyes. His three central eyes were dead and looked like plaques of dried-up skin, and he had an expansive abdomen, bloated and taut, which pulled him backward and made all his movement clumsy and ridiculous.

"Greeny, you're kind of strange," said the grey mantis. "As if you're not really here, but somewhere else. Are you high on something?"

"No," Lena answered. "Let's not talk, Misha."

"Fine," the grey mantis agreed.

And they started dancing the dance that engenders new life.

As soon as it was over, Lena followed the promptings of the ageless wisdom. She squeezed Botvinik's head tightly between her spiky hands and tugged hard.

"Are you crazy?" the stupid grey mantis hissed and started flailing at her with its feeble little forelegs. But Lena's body was covered with a strong chitinous shell and she didn't feel their touch. The grey mantis's head was hard to tear off, because its neck was very thick, but Lena could feel an insuperable, steely strength in her hands, and she knew that sooner or later she would finish the job.

The girls started singing the national anthem of the USSR in English—the Paul Robeson version. Uncle Pete was fond of saying that there was something boundlessly orgiastic about this rendering, and praised it as the best possible background music for VIP intimate relations. Lena heard three frightened voices singing:

Strong in our friendship tried by fire,
Long may our crimson flag inspire ...

They were singing exactly like Paul Robeson—they'd learned the number from his old recording—articulating the r in "fire" and "inspire" forcefully, in a way that is rarely done in English. Somehow it was that rolling r that helped: Lena braced herself and twisted the grey mantis's head as sharply as she could.

"Ee-ikh," the grey mantis whispered, the central sinew of his being yielded, and he went limp forever.

Lena saw how the part of the great river that had been locked inside him was released in a jet of dark smoke, like car exhaust fumes—it was instantly swept somewhere downwards. Lena followed it in her mind and sensed a swirling, somber crimson space, with grim voices rumbling remorselessly: "Who do you think you're calling a faggot, you cunt? Who are you telling to get fucked?" There were other voices too—quiet, shrewdly insinuating, and really creepy, saying things like: "Spiralwise with cabbage, sixteen, forty-two ..." That gave Lena a bad feeling, and she stopped following the smoke's descent. She now had to hurry, and started twisting the grey mantis's head from side to side as rapidly as she could.

Botvinik's head had still not come away from his body when Lena realized she had passed the exam: once again she saw the happy meadow, flooded with trembling, shimmering sunlight. Two large praying mantises were hurrying toward her to assist in making the crossing. They were clutching two special chattering sticks in their forelegs, using them to help her shrug off her human body forever. Although it was a bit painful, she knew the pain would disappear forever with the body.

"I wonder what's inside me?" she thought. "Could it really be that same grey, stinking stuff? Well, now we'll find out.... No, it's not the same. There, look at it. It's bright ... luminous ... pure.... It's so very beautiful...."

Victor Pelevin

"Mr. Pelevin is certainly an unusual and strange writer, one with the kind of mordant, astringent turn of mind that in the pre-glasnost era landed writers in psychiatric hospitals or exile." —*The New York Times*

"Victor Pelevin is the real article: a writer whose imagination dances on the heads of the rustiest pins in history, while maintaining a likably zany manner." —*San Francisco Bay Guardian*

"A master absurdist, a brilliant satirist of things Soviet, but also of things human." —*Spin*

Born in Moscow in 1962, **Victor Pelevin** got a degree in electromechanical engineering from the Moscow Power Engineering Institute before studying at the Maxim Gorky Literature Institute. Pelevin's first story was published in 1989 and his collection *The Blue Lantern* won the Russian Little Booker Prize. A notorious media recluse, Pelevin prefers to spend time in Buddhist monastery retreats when he is not writing. A journalist once invited him to lunch and secretly recorded and published their entire conversation. In 2006 Pelevin posted all his published work up to that point online. His latest novel, *Pineapple Water for a Beautiful Lady*, was published in Russia in 2010.